To

Thanks for your
encouragement and help

Gratefully

Ferg.

PLEASE DON'T GET SICK

PLEASE DON'T GET SICK

Albert Barnett Ferguson Jr., M.D.,
FRCS (Lond.) Hon., FACS

VANTAGE PRESS
New York

FIRST EDITION

All rights reserved, including the right of
reproduction in whole or in part in any form.

Copyright © 1996 by Albert Barnett Ferguson Jr., M.D.

Published by Vantage Press, Inc.
516 West 34th Street, New York, New York 10001

Manufactured in the United States of America
ISBN: 0-533-11745-3

Library of Congress Catalog Card No.: 95-90863

0 9 8 7 6 5 4 3 2 1

To Sanford, Bruce, Gary, and Laurie

Contents

Background	xi
Acknowledgements	xiii
Introduction	xv
I. Medicine as a Business	1
The Physician	3
Tinkering with Health Care	3
Why Health Care Arose as a Political Issue	4
The Case of Blue Cross	5
II. A Maturing Medical Care Society	9
The Making of the New Physician: Antibiotics	10
Increasing Technology in Medical Care	12
Public Health Evaluations of Medical Practice	13
Public Health Surveys of Medical Practice	15
Problems Paying for Health Care	16
The Canadian Plan	19
The Nursing Profession	20
III. Medical Practice Today	25
Criteria for the Insurance Company's Choice of Physician	25
Don't Diagnose; Just Treat Symptoms: A Recipe for Disaster	26
Medical Care Today	28
The Nursing Profession	29
A Sample Patient Progression Today: Will Green's Story	31
The Gatekeeper Concept and the HMOs	35
The Annual Physical	38
Referral	38

Career Choice—Medicine Becomes Corporate Practice	39
Corporations Practicing Medicine	40
The Emergency Room	41
Intensive Care Beds	43
The HMO	44
IV. Medicine for the Future	47
The Patient and the Doctor	47
Capitalism, Computers, and Kemeny	50
How Socialized Medicine Spawns Private Health Care Insurance	53
Extraordinary Medical Efforts Arise to Combat Dictatorships	55
Society Needs Scientists	57
A Science Needs a Humanitarian to Render Maximum Service to Society	57
A Poor State Improves Its Medical Care	59
Managed Care Is, First, a Business	60
Women Find Their Place in Medicine	62
Trustees and Research	64
Funding From NIH	65
V. Trying to Find the Answer	69
Institutional Overhead	69
The Need for Institutional Support	71
Medicine Benefits from Hard Workers	73
Fundamentals Still Matter in Efficient Medical Practice	76
Specialization Is Necessary in Medical Practice	77
Deteriorating Health Care—Progressing Fast	78
VI. A Solution so We Can Get Sick Again	81
A Unit Cost for Medical Care	81
Paying for Medical Care	84

A Solution so We Can Get Sick Again	87
Managed Care Runs into Legal Limitations	89
Managed-Care Solutions	91
The Growth of Managed Care	97
Deficits of the System	98

Background

It takes a broad exposure to all the facets of health care in order to write a book about the massive changes taking place in the system in the United States. Some aspects deny the patients the care they need. Some aspects prevent the physician from delivering care at the level the patient needs.

The background of the author was principally as chairman of the Department of Orthopaedics at the University of Pittsburgh. This included a large practice with patients from all walks of life. It included children, athletes, ballet stars, hard workers from the mills, home services, and individuals working two and three jobs at once. The practice included arthritis and the placement of artificial joints.

He was a member of council of an institute at the National Institutes of Health that covered arthritis, diabetes, gastrointestinal disease, dermatology, and orthopaedic surgery. He was a member of the board of Blue Cross of Western Pennsylvania for fourteen years, the chairman of the executive committee of Presbyterian-University Hospital for eighteen years and the president of the American Orthopaedic Association and the American Board of Orthopaedic Surgery. He saw the penniless and the rich. He had a front row seat on the development of sports medicine and the use of the arthroscope.

In forty years he enjoyed a great experience with many facets of medicine. After retirement he watched the changes take place with the corporate invasion of medicine and the imposition of managed health care.

The experience made him want to acquaint patients and physicians with what was happening to their world.

Acknowledgements

There was a lot of encouragement from friends, physicians, and former patients, who urged me on to write this book. One, Robert Atwell, a superb and busy surgeon, told me a revealing story involving an executive of a managed health care plan.

Dr. Atwell had two patients in the hospital at the same time in adjoining rooms. One had colon cancer, and his operation involved resecting his cancer and reconstructing his bowel. Across the hall the other patient was the CEO of an insurance company selling managed-care health insurance. "You know," he said to Dr. Atwell, "you have done a disservice to the cause of managed care. You operated on that man across the hall for colon cancer. You know that statistics show that after five years patients with that diagnosis have a mortality rate of 90 percent. You could have treated him symptomatically at much less cost." Dr. Atwell had difficulty digesting this underlying philosophy.

I have had help from many friends who enabled me to produce this book. The book is based on personal experiences while having a medical career that spanned thirty years. The manuscript was read by Thomas Brower, a philosopher and teacher, who is now retired from the chair of orthopaedic surgery at the University of Kentucky. Stan Williams, the retired CEO of the PPG Corporation, critiqued the manuscript as well. Bill Appel, a professional writer, edited and improved the work.

My internist, protégé and friend, F. X. Solano, volunteered the title, *Please Don't Get Sick,* from his own letter to his patients. Mary Cosgrove, my secretary of over thirty years, typed and retyped the enlarging manuscript. My wife, Louise, was a proofreader trying to improve the quality of the writing.

Patients and those concerned with health care costs may learn how important it is to maintain quality in medicine and how the imposition of new health care systems now threatens a valuable resource that we have had up till now.

Introduction

Please don't get sick! This is a plea from the country's doctors. Since I am a retired orthopaedic surgeon it has become evident that both doctors and patients are in the midst of a massive revolution that affects how physicians deliver care and what level of care patients will receive. It is also evident that this revolution is substituting lesser levels of care for that which was formerly available. As a physician I want to expose how this change is occurring and make it evident with anecdotes describing how physicians acted in the past.

There are forces afoot to reduce the availability of well-trained specialists. Managed care furnished by insurance companies is placing impediments in the way of the patient's ability to seek high levels of care. It is time to assess the organization of medical care that is occurring. These broad movements try to use methods that reduce costs.

This book is one man's description of how we are putting a national treasure at risk. The national treasure is the ability to save lives, reconstruct bodies, restore function, and make life a meaningful experience. It is called our present-day practice of medicine.

Don't get sick or the losses that have occurred in the excellence of medical practice that we have already suffered will become apparent. Managed health care plans offer "distinctive" medicine to the patient. The methods these plans use to provide lower cost include using lesser levels of care formerly done at a higher level. The plan may not include the best physicians; there may be economic penalties for both the physician who tries to provide health care and the patient who tries to receive it.

A gatekeeper who may not have a medical background may be interposed between the patient and the providers of care. This may lead to inaccurate or delayed treatment.

At this moment there is still a supply of well-trained specialists. It is essential to preserve the pipeline that produced these individuals. The disincentives now choking off the entrance of intelligent individuals into a mainstream that leads to further education and training are very effective. The medical community can gradually run out of exceptionally gifted individuals and the patients may find themselves in treatment modes where the least-trained physicians are expected to do it all.

The future in medicine is not hard to predict if the planning for medical care is done by individuals without a medical background.

Keep the Good Guys

Those who live in the United States are leaving many decades of excellent medical care behind them. In these decades the physicians were available at all hours in their day. There are many pressures that can be explained as this book progresses that lead to a "nine-to-four" doctor. At other times in the twenty-four-hour day a scheduled assistant is being made available. These assistants have been taught technical tasks. As examples, blood pressure can be taken, needles can be inserted into veins, and serious deterioration of the patient's condition can be measured. A professional training that leads to diagnosis and appropriate treatment is not immediately available.

This is an approach that has been used in managed societies such as that in Russia. There the population has been told that there is a doctor's office in each block of the city of Moscow. This care level is not what has been available in the United States. There is, of course, another level of care and separate institutions for the party elite.

In the late sixties two young planners addressing the problem of sufficient medical care for the population predicted a shortage of 50,000 physicians in the United States. The medical background of these planners was immature and done by individuals who may have had an M.D. degree but had never experienced medical practice. Senators Proxmire and Edward Kennedy led a charge with measures to overcome this projected physician shortage. The output of physicians was doubled, but the training was not raised to a higher level.

West Virginia received funds for four new medical schools due to the effectiveness of Senator Byrd. The first of these schools opened in Morgantown, West Virginia. There was not a big-enough patient population to support the training of medical students, so they had to rotate through another new school in Charlestown, West Virginia. Faculty recruitment was very difficult for both these schools. There were funds still coming so two additional schools were opened. In Huntington, West Virginia, the school was based in the Veteran's Administration Hospital. A state-supported VA osteopathic school was opened in Lewisburg, West Virginia. In retrospect this state would have had trouble supporting just one medical school and providing capable basic scientists to educate the students to a high level. The number of individuals receiving a doctorate in medicine increased, but it was questionable that the medical care level had been increased.

The number of doctors was increased by the addition of

twelve new medical schools spread over the country. An escalation in medical costs also occurred during the same period. This may have been due to the increased technology involved in medical care. However, one senator (whom I cannot identify, although I remember his words) said, "We have increased the number of doctors by 100,000 and the cost of medical care has gone up and you the voters are surprised. Would you be surprised if we turned loose 100,000 criminals that the crime rate went up?"

Those who live in the United States have benefitted from the development of the highest standards of medical care in the world. I don't want to pressure for tradition's sake, but we need a solution to our medical care cost that allows the lowering of cost but the maintenance of the excellence in care that the United States has enjoyed.

I have made suggestions that will keep our great population from throwing everything out of our old system and yet diminish the cost of medical care. It is evident that patients cannot be at risk by having their care determined by health plans using managed care as a tool. The stock of managed health-care plans is a favorite investment right now because these plans are making money. The question naturally arises: At whose expense?

This book is not a defense of earlier medical practice. It does criticize those who would turn medicine into a corporate-run machine in which physicians' ideals have little input and the patients' welfare is not the primary goal. It is possible to end up with the treatment of the elderly called economically irrational and substitute machine scanning for personal examination. Medical practice in the future may substitute the treatment of symptoms for the care of disease conditions based on physical diagnosis of the disease and using the appropriate treatment. So much has been done to accurately recognize disease and use the tools that medical science has provided that the disappearance of good medical practice should scare the well-being of everyone.

I am trying to give examples that convey, accurately, what it was that made medical practice a valuable resource. This carries with it as a problem to be overcome the modes and modalities that are threatening the continuation of a valuable resource.

PLEASE DON'T GET SICK

Chapter I
Medicine as a Business

The liquid assets of health management organizations have increased by 15 percent or more in the past year (1995). This amounts to over one billion dollars or more for many of those individual organizations. This inflow of cash occurs because membership is growing. Most of this is in large corporate groups who have bought managed health care plans because they have offered lower cost.

How are these health plans able to lower cost? They have selected doctors for their panels on the basis of lowering their cost. I would feel more comfortable if these physicians had been selected on the basis of training, skill, and patient rapport. What criteria did the plan use? Doctors are as confused as you are. There is a strong possibility that the available physicians for the managed-care panel are likely to be those least sought by patients previously.

There are other reasons for lowering health care costs. It is not healthy for patients that having a baby entitles them to a one-day recovery. People vary, deliveries vary, and complications vary. The whole process cannot be subjected to a rigid administrator based on cost. It is possible to compare any condition requiring hospitalization to the same analysis.

The use of rationing to lower health care costs is too tempting for health care plans to avoid. It is a given that rationing will be disguised. The use of a gatekeeper is a means to achieve rationing and it is hard to find a plan without it. The general practitioner is not fond of being placed in a gatekeeper position. Even the gatekeeper must deal with the keeper of the purse at the insurance company desk. These decisions are often made on nonmedical grounds. If you have a serious medical condition, it is not often immediately apparent. A skilled diagnostician may be necessary.

Hospitals themselves can tighten up their practices to reduce cost, and hospital costs have become a bear with whom it is hard to discern reality. This is an aspect that will require a more detailed inspection to be reviewed as the book progresses.

The dispensing of medicine can be made more accurate and with avoidance of human error. Here modern robot technology not only can reduce error but also eliminate the hiring of unnecessary hands. The hospital pharmacy is becoming automated. The initial cost of the medicine is a bargaining process between the manufacturer and the hospital.

There are duplicated costs in areas such as anesthesia and radiology. The professional fee is one cost, but many hospitals incorporate a professional cost in their fee as well. I'll try to examine many of these practices further in this book.

Physicians had difficulty understanding why they should be excluded from the formulation of a socialized medical program formulated by the government. The formulation of the program, as seen by the committee named by the government, was voluminous and lacked insight into the realities of medical practice..It contained coercion to make the citizens adhere to the plan. It was difficult to understand and consequently failed to gain support.

In evaluating health care plans, whether run by the government or by private industry, the patient should be able to determine how a free choice of physician will be obtained.

The Physician

It is apparent that some doctors must specialize after their initial entry into the system. The reason is because medicine is so complex that it is beyond any one physician's ability to comprehend it all. It was recognized in years past that specialization can increase speed, efficiency, and lower the cost of care. There is no greater waste in medical care than to have a curable disease that has been followed for months with inappropriate care.

As a patient you need not only a physician who has been educated and trained to recognize your problem but one who can reach you by communicating with you sufficiently so that you, the patient, and the doctor understand each other clearly.

Physicians who reached the patients they saw with their warmth and concern and their command of the skills of their profession were much sought after in years gone by. Other physicians recognized these attributes in their fellows and referred patients to them. Patients who experienced care that caused them to broadcast rave reviews of their service were also a source of referral. It was not unusual for a physician to find that the major source of patient referrals was other patients.

The confidence that permits you to undergo medical care with peace of mind will have some difficulty getting into your consciousness no matter how skilled the corporate advertiser unless you, the patient, have determined who you wish to take care of you.

Tinkering with Health Care

If we can tinker with the system to correct those things

that we perceive as doing harm and yet avoid destroying the good care that we perceive we have then we must be intelligent about our approach. Many people want to change our health care system and its insurance into a less costly system. You can guess that politicians were attracted to the possible voter support that could arise from the proposition.

Harris Wofford won an election in Pennsylvania by bringing up health care as an issue. He did not have a plan, but he did have an opponent who left him an opening. The reason he won was based on more than using health care as an issue; however, political pundits blamed Governor Thornburgh's loss on the airing of this by Wofford.

The basis for voters wanting to change our health care system is not because when they were sick they did not get good care. People wanted ongoing coverage of possible calamitous health care costs when they changed jobs. People have always wanted protection against medical calamity costs and have demonstrated this desire for fifty years. This was evident in the initial formation of Blue Cross. It seems more and more apparent that when insurance companies or the government become the dispenser of medical coverage costs then rationing will be involved. That we need more information about how the medical system works is evident to both patient and doctor. If we do not have this information, then we can destroy the medical care we have, lose our choice of doctor, and destroy the incentives that have given us world-class care.

Why Health Care Arose as a Political Issue

The politicians are trying to catch the health care train as it thunders by. What they caught onto was the caboose. As a result they are being jerked about in many directions to a destination they are unaware of. The political capital they hope to make may be at great cost to the United States. It may also cost the politicians dearly since they have so little understanding of how we achieved a medical care system that brings people to our shores from other world populations. It may cost the public dearly since there is so little understanding of the flaws that do stand the need for improvement, correction, or obliteration. It takes great effort to preserve the high level of medical care that we have achieved. Unless the public understands this area of our life it will wake up without it.

The attempt to change how we pay for our medical care did not begin with the physicians. When corporations took on the expense of medical care for their employees they were unaware of how much it would eventually cost. To remedy their own balance sheet they began seeking relief by achieving the underwriting of this cost by the government. They were already paying for the medical care with pretax dollars.

The Case of Blue Cross

The need for change became apparent twenty years ago. It began when major corporations gave in to a union demand for underwriting the health care of its members as a union benefit. The government ruled this expense as a nontaxable expense on the corporate balance sheet. U.S. Steel was presented with a demand for a total underwriting of the health care needs of union members by the United Steel Workers.

There had been lesser forays into this area in the past, but without being included in the contract. This time it was big and nationwide. Blue Cross of Western Pennsylvania was located in Pittsburgh as were the headquarters of U.S. Steel and the United Steel Workers. Since the headquarters of all three were in Pittsburgh and communication was easy, a nationwide contract could be written from this location.

At this juncture Blue Cross was only a vehicle charging approximately 5 percent overhead to carry out the mission of reimbursement of health care services provided to U.S. Steel's union members. U.S. Steel paid the cost of this service by reimbursing Blue Cross. U.S. Steel had no oversight of this process in terms of riding hard on costs. The union had only one aim for the member benefit: that no member should bear any cost for his or her health care.

There was no deterrent to the use of this Blue Cross contract. There was no deterrent for the consumer. There was no deterrent for the provider. Large sums of money were involved. The money was enough to turn nonprofit provider hospitals into profitable institutions. It was enough to affect corporate balance sheets as the cost for health care benefits rose rapidly to 30 percent of the corporate balance sheets. Once health care became a union benefit on this grand a scale, other businesses were forced to follow suit, so that a no-cost union benefit for health care was widely used in strike demands and achieved widespread success.

I can remember sitting at the board table of Blue Cross of Western Pennsylvania proposing some sort of copay and being told by the union representative this was not negotiable. The corporation had given in to this demand without any safeguards, either in control of hospital costs or in controlling unwarranted use of medical care facilities by providers or the excessive use by union members.

What happened from this point on, either in the change of Blue Cross from an agency to collect and disburse funds with a low overhead to a corporation making a profit out of medical care or in hospitals growing into profitable enterprises is an intriguing story: Hospital administration began a major role in determining what medical care the institution would provide. Administration, as a cost on the hospital balance sheet, rose from 9 percent in the 1960s to over 35 percent of hospital costs twenty-five years later. The physician continued to receive nineteen cents on the health care dollar, with 50 percent of that money going for overhead, such as employees, rent, and supplies.

Health care benefits, through an insurance contract, became a standard benefit of employment. The tools of health care providers became increasingly sophisticated and expensive. Hospital administrators saw their income rise with the hospitals' cash flow.

Hospital board members saw it as their duty to provide all forms of medical care and medical devices at their hospitals.

The board members were very cognizant of the need to maintain a positive balance sheet. There was no way for hospital costs to go but up. There had to be duplication among the providers. Each hospital felt that they were competing against their neighbors. Either provide a magnetic resonance installation or a heart surgery team or lose patients to their competitors was the dilemma hospitals faced.

Chapter II
A Maturing Medical Care Society

In 1953 I received reimbursement for no more than 70 percent of the work I did. There were so many people needing help that the possibility of future payment never occurred to me while undertaking any patient's care. There were viable collection agencies, and when a salesman for one of these agencies approached years later I was not emotionally ready to hire him. The thought of a stranger totally uninvolved in the care of a patient approaching someone who was struggling with his bills, employment, injury, or disease was an ugly one to me.

I was not the richest doctor in town, but I could pay the cost of my home and my children and as long as these were not threatened I could hardly collect from anyone else. Other physicians felt that if the plumber expected to be paid, they should have the same expectation. Somehow this cast a pall over the work that physicians enjoyed. I enjoyed the dependence the patients had on me and the fact that I could help. My greatest disappointment came when I did not or could not help. In my relationship with patients we did not discuss cost because I knew that they would not have to pay if they could not. I warned them, however, especially as the years wore on, that the hospital did not have a leeway of forgiveness for charges and that dealing with that institution would be tougher. It was also true that the hospital had some very considerate people working in the cashier's office who would interview the patient to work out a feasible plan of repayment.

When reimbursement from insurance came along, the physician changed and so did the hospital. Physicians had to hire additional staff just to handle insurance forms.

The first time I noticed a change was when John L. Lewis introduced his plan to provide medical care for miners. God knows the miners needed a plan for care. John L. Lewis was an idealist, but he was not blessed with an administrator's staff able to keep his plan economically viable. But this plan brought up many problems in a world where physicians' roles were changing. Companies were now arising who wanted to make money from medical care.

Physicians were subject to influences that formerly did not exist. The majority of the fees for their services now came from plans that provided medical coverage for patients' care. In many cases this coverage now reimbursed the physician for services that formerly were rendered without charge. Some of the good feeling in physicians' hearts began to vanish as formerly free patients were often compensated for.

This and the growth in previously unknown medicines and the increasing technical aid that was available began to move the physicians further away from the patient.

The Making of the New Physician: Antibiotics

Unless the physician had experienced the practice of medicine before the advent of penicillin the changes in the practice of medicine would be unbelievable.

The arrival of antibiotics reshaped the profile of young doctors. The broad coverage of these new tools lessened the necessity for accurate diagnosis.

Before World War II people died of pneumonia. Syphilis and gonorrhea were treatable only in the crudest, most painful and unsuccessful way. Osteomyelitis was not regularly curable. Appendicitis led to the demise of otherwise healthy young adults. It is hard to comprehend the extent that family members suffered from the loss of cherished individuals in the 1930s because we could not overcome bacterial infection.

Now we expect to control these threats to our continued life. The problem for medical practitioners is to continue to have available antibiotics that target specific organisms. As bacteria adjust their metabolism to become immune, the problem is one in which research scientists must continue to develop new antibiotics faster than the organism can develop defenses against them. Penicillin, which was the major instigator of this new world, came about through a chance occurrence that may not be duplicated.

Penicillin's arrival came about through a change that was noted in an open petri dish where bacteria had settled and started to grow. Fleming, working in England in a hospital laboratory with wooden benches and dusty window sills, noted a clear zone about colonies of bacteria. This fortunate observation led to work to determine what was occupying the clear zone in which bacteria could not grow.

Since the penicillin that was isolated was new to the bacteria, it initially proved very efficient. The broad coverage of its action in inhibiting bacterial growth lessened the need for accurate diagnosis. The new physician turned to other aspects of an old disease. Drug companies in particular increased their outlay for research in the development of still other types of antibiotics. The hospital stay of the affected patient was shortened, the mortality reduced, and in some ways, the physician lessened medicine's interest in ancillary therapeutic measures. The new physician could go home confident that the patient's disease was going to be controlled.

Increasing Technology in Medical Care

Medicine's attention could turn to increasingly complicated and technical methods to diagnosing other conditions. These methods and tools were the product of the advent of computer technology that could be applied to values obtained by automated chemical analysis or the use of magnetic resonance, which diminished the need for the use of X-ray exposure.

The values obtained by the use of automation could be printed in the patient's chart for the physician's inspection and interpretation. Medicine became increasingly technical, and diagnoses became more accurate. It followed that therapy became more appropriate and the results or treatment became more successful.

It is not necessary to use these machine scans with their computer interpretation on every patient. Many diagnoses can still be made by the old-fashioned history and physical examination. It becomes important to avoid using scanning techniques on every patient with a headache to see if a brain tumor or cerebral hemorrhage exists. These machines require a multimillion-dollar outlay to obtain.

Two forces come to bear on their use. The first is competition from the other centers and the second is the medical-legal whip that the legal profession has in their armamentarium. This has spawned the development of groups of physicians who are professional testifiers. The increased technology enlarges the possible scope of its use. It increased the cost of medical care and spurs the need for an evaluation by the legal profession of the extent to which the failure to use the technology on every patient can be labeled malpractice. This will not occur unless the financial reward changes. It is one of the factors in the increased cost of medical care at the present time. If the new physician neglects the time-honored use of the physical examination to aid in making diagnoses but turns instead to increased use of technology, the methods of medicine will not simplify. The growth of legal analysis of medicine's methods by the legal profession will continue since it is financially rewarding. This medical-legal approach affects physician behavior.

These are also evaluations of medical care that receive widespread publicity. The patient is familiar with the changing pronouncements that reach the press regarding the effect of butter or oleomargarine on cholesterol levels in the patient's body.

There are other pronouncements on the necessity of medical care that often originate in the world of evaluation by public health physicians. Many of these evaluations have not had the benefit of medical practice and patient relationships that enter into these evaluations.

Public Health Evaluations of Medical Practice

There apparently was a group of interns in a Worcester, Massachusetts, hospital who were striking to get rid of night call. Commitment to medical school should mean a commitment to what is involved in the practice of medicine. Entrance into medical school is not done with blinders on the applicant. It may be true that many become doctors for the wrong reasons. Medicine is, after all, primarily a service occupation, interpreting and employing scientific advances. For some individuals the commitment to clinical medical practice is not an option that can be used when they find themselves unable to tolerate the demands of this life.

In my experience most public health physicians went to medical school but found that they did not enjoy meeting patients face to face. As a result they sought alternatives to medical practice. The selection of medical students who could enter the field where patient contact is a requirement must be made by evaluations at the time of selection. If the process relies too heavily on the grades achieved in scientific subjects then some will be admitted who cannot reach or enjoy the patient and lack sympathy with the patient's predicament.

The entrance into the reality of medical practice is difficult for some individuals. They must answer to the demands of the patient. They must be on call regardless of their personal schedule. They must answer the telephone's insistent ring. They must explain, comfort, and be understanding without regard to their other commitments. There are many graduates of medical school who cannot handle these demands and are not suited to it so they seek other avenues where they can make use of their medical background.

Fields such as radiology and pathology lessen personal contact with the patient. Public health careers divorce the individual from dealing with the patient. In the field of public health, patients now become statistics and work hours become regular without phone call interruptions. Judgments can be made on the basis of statistics, but leaving out patients' reactions to their disease conditions skews these statistics. The interpretation of results needs to include the patient's disability before and after treatment. The judgment as to this disability cannot be done from a desk, but needs direct face-to-face patient-physician interaction throughout the course of the disease.

Public Health Surveys of Medical Practice

I have commented on the weakness of surveys of results by those far removed from the treatment problem. The criteria for necessary or unnecessary surgery, for example, must include how the disease affected the patient's enjoyment and function in life. It cannot be based solely on the presence or absence of cancer, for instance.

I have conjured up a few examples of the way such officials' isolation from everyday medicine distorts their views of public policy.

Evaluations of Medical Practice

If I take a commonly used criticism of medical practice we can use the example of hysterectomy (removal of the uterus). These critiques regularly appear in newspaper articles. A large percentage of hysterectomies are deemed by the public health experts to be unnecessary. The criteria used is: if the uterus contains cancer, it is necessary; if it does not, it is unnecessary. If these evaluations were practiced in the world of females over forty (past child-bearing age) they would have to confront women with chronic backache. These patients feel enormous pressure on the pelvic support ligaments when standing. The boggy, distended uterus is no longer supported by an intact pelvic floor. The enjoyment of life is affected after child bearing, which has stretched the support for the pelvic organs so that gravity stretches these ligaments still farther. An interview with patients trying to be functional with this condition reveals that there are reasons why women seek relief from carrying the weight of a boggy, distended uterus. There are other reasons for patients' complaints other than cancer of the uterus for considering the restructuring of pelvic weight bearing and hysterectomy in order to achieve a more comfortable life.

In males the prostate is an organ that undergoes change with advancing age. It is rare to find a male over seventy who does not have some type of cancerous change in the prostate. In addition, the prostate is placed in a position to shut off the ability to pass urine, an ability that we cannot live without.

There is more to this problem than whether the organ has cancer. The judgment as to whether prostate surgery is necessary is a considered opinion involving the patient and his complaints, with the surgeon as an interpreter and patient educator. It involves more than a public health official's judgment as to what is necessary or unnecessary. The public health official does not have to deal with these patient complaints. The study has to include more than statistics on the incidence of cancer.

There are complaints related to the prostate having to do with the ability to urinate. There are complaints related to the ability to maintain an erection and continue with an active sex life. Again the criteria that make the operations necessary are not solely related to the presence or absence of cancer. This is not the sole attribute for the patient. Familiarity with the clinical conditions of the patient could lead to a different set of statistical values when a judgment of necessary or unnecessary is being made.

Problems Paying for Health Care

The United Mine Workers established clinics throughout their working area. They were able to hire idealistic physicians and surgeons at very low cost. These individuals were well educated and able. When the patient's problem necessitated the use of special knowledge and skill, other doctors were used on a piece-work basis. In western Pennsylvania this resulted in physicians being paid for work that they formerly did for no compensation. There were those who felt that they should be paid at the highest private-practice rate even though their gross income had risen due to coverage for those who formerly were treated for free. The United Mine Workers quickly discovered who was milking the system and who was treating their practice plan fairly. Referral was made to those who had earned a good reputation with the administrators of the plan but who also had a reputation for skill in which they felt confidence. The clinics had a hard time surviving in a financial sense. Many physicians felt that these patients should be treated at a lesser rate in view of the now-guaranteed reimbursement. Unfortunately, this view was not shared by all practitioners. The Mine Workers Union clinic did not ration the services provided to patients. This was another reason for their declining finances. It was a nice trial but very hard to bring to reality. The expense was more than anyone anticipated. It was the forerunner of care plans and was high in idealism, low in realism, and pointed out the difficulties of those who entered into the underwriting of health care as a business.

Everyone wants to make medical care less costly. The four major ways to do this are:

1. Rationing (a component of every medical care plan that has ever been tried).
2. Substituting inexpensive care for the highest level of care. The Russians made a simple change to fill this requirement. The "doctors" were really just technicians.
3. Changing the way physicians are paid by negotiating contracts at the lowest possible cost. Physi-

cians are not used to bonding together in these situations.
4. Making lower-cost contracts based on volume. This applies to drugs, laundry, food, and labor.

The plan may guarantee the physician a given number of patients and pay a set fee for the care of each individual. This is referred to as capitation. The physician is paid the set fee on a monthly basis. The monthly fee may vary from $6 to $15 per month, depending on the patient's age. This fee is for the generalist who also functions as a gatekeeper. The patient often pays a fee of less than $5 per month as a copayment. Bonuses may be provided to the physician as the use of tests is reduced. There is no incentive to provide care. There is more phone medicine and more care provided by ancillary personnel. If the patient has no incentive or financial risk for their own care the provider may be run ragged.

It doesn't matter who provides the medical care underwriting, whether it be health insurance companies or government underwriting using the meaningless term "HMO" for their policies. The equally meaningless term "managed care" is used in order to mask old-fashioned rationing.

Either way, major decisions about your health care are going to be made by administrators working at a desk well removed from you, the patient. The guiding consideration is the bottom line. Forms of medical care that affect the quality of life may not be available to you. Age may become a criterion used to determine whether a particular treatment is available to you. Lesser care encourages treatment without diagnosis provided by nurse technicians; pain clinics; special approaches broadly applied by chiropractors; heat, light, and exercise management; and physiotherapy regimes aimed at reducing symptoms.

The Canadian Plan

In Canada the original Canadian medical system is not the system those citizens now have. When the medical care system started there was a "means test." In rough terms, the portion of the population falling into the lowest 20 percent in terms of income was treated without charge. The middle income group of 60 percent had a shared charge. The upper 20 percent, in income terms, paid the full bill entirely. There were many problems since government employees made decisions affecting medical care, but at least the system could be supported by Canada's high taxes.

For a politician an easy way to gain votes was to increase the lower-income group by definition. They enlarged the number of individuals for whom medical care was entirely covered. The tax base could not afford this additional expense. Before long the system was bankrupt and unable to survive as a full-care entity. The pressure to save money led to limitation of services. In these circumstances the system could not afford the major medical advances available to patients in the United States.

Some doctors left Canada for areas where medical care and modern machinery used in medicine was available. The physicians who left had built reputations for excellence that made them sought after by institutions in the United States. The quality of leadership in medicine diminished in Canada as a result. The bureaucrats who ran the system were forced to increasingly substitute a lesser quality of care for the individuals in the least-pay group. A once proud medical plan was forced to offer less care to those who were ill.

Interestingly, those gifts of the government that were obvious in their political value remained. The helping home services continued, such as nursing care visits and physiotherapy.

Those who felt the diminishing support for operations that would improve the quality of life were the elderly. A division of patients between the elderly with the most medical care demands and the young who had fewer illnesses and greater ability to surmount their health care needs arose. The young felt adequately covered; the elderly felt deprived. The governmental provision for medical care does not affect the young enough for them to be concerned. Except where elderly members of a family were involved, the young did not feel the deficiencies in the system.

The Nursing Profession

For the first time in memory the demand for nurses to fill supervisory positions in hospital-care routine has slackened. The underlying reason is cost. The nurses have priced themselves out of the market. The personalities of nurses that were exceptional can be illustrated by descriptions of their activity in the past compared to the routine in today's world. These are selected examples that make the point. Susan Wargo is a type that has vanished.

Susan Wargo

Susan Wargo was as broad as she was tall, which made her five feet by five feet or twenty-five square feet of jollies for the children and dedicated to their care. Visiting cowboys, football heroes, and actors and actresses would stop on her orthopaedic floor when they visited Children's Hospital in Pittsburgh. Every weekday when the Pittsburgh Pirates were in town some would make a morning stop in groups of two or three on their way to the ballpark.

Susan did not have a Ph.D. in nursing, although under pressure from the Nursing Department she eventually obtained a Master's degree. She was the most dedicated, hardest working bedpan nurse I have ever seen. She grew up in the age of bedside nursing, and the bedside is where she could be found. She did not have an office but took reports from the fellow workers at the nurses' desk with all the charts open in front of her. She practically had a computer in her head because she could instantly tell you on rounds when a medication had been given and how much.

Susan had a great ability to handle and repair mechanical things. She understood that prolonged local pressure could lead to complications with nerves and arteries and stop their function. She caught possible disasters before they occurred because she was there on the floor going from bed to bed.

Susan Wargo was forced to retire as a head nurse when a better educated nurse took the executive position from the floor and into the nursing office. The skills that had been so useful on an orthopaedic floor included a natural bent into mechanical things. While Susan was busy on the orthopaedic ward she found time during World War II to take a course to qualify as an automobile mechanic. She mastered this skill as well, and after the war she drove her car up to the AlCan Highway and did her own repairs along the way. Her mechanical skills had previously made an additional contribution to the war effort. This was indicative of the sense of duty that she carried into her work.

In the hospital, work still included the necessity to carry the bedpan away. This task was gradually passed down to the least responsibile person, who frequently was cognizant of the condition of the patient to a greater degree than the head nurse, who no longer appeared at the bedside.

The nurse gradually became supervisor of the less

skilled worker. The number of degree-bearing nurses on a working shift declined. The number of nurse's aides increased. The involvement of the head nurse now became limited to the supervisory desk.

The cost of nursing care has risen as those with advanced degrees became more numerous. The knowledge of psychology has improved, but time to use it at the bedside has declined as the nurse is pestered by forms and records that must be completed before the shift is over. The changes were evident in out-patient as well as in-patient care. The career of Katie Greatrix illustrates the out-patient scene as supervision of the work moved back into the office and nurses were supplanted by aides.

Katie Greatrix

When hospital functions became an administrative nightmare and physicians had a diminishing voice in these functions there was a loss of both heart and efficiency. The career of Katie Greatrix can serve as an illustration because she possessed a caring attitude and the ability to entertain. She was in the working area and knew how the materials were used and was very familiar with a physician's ability.

The orthopaedic outpatient and the cast room where casts were applied and minor fractures were treated was Katie's domain. Katie was an outgoing, humorous person who found that her life centered around the kids who were treated in the cast room and the orthopaedic outpatient at Children's Hospital.

The kids who lay on the table had nothing to see but a white ceiling while they wondered what the doctors were going to do. The day-to-day physicians were young residents in their first five years of professional growth after internship and medical school. They grew to idolize Katie. She was interested in transmitting the emotional concern of medicine that she had observed in the chief of the orthopaedic service. She had learned how plaster should be applied to make a trouble-free cast. She knew the pitfalls produced when lack of skill led to pressure sores from a poorly made cast. She knew what type of plaster rolls could be applied on different sizes of patients and what was necessary to avoid damage from water and failure to support and elevate the limb encased in the cast. This cast was soon initialed by the physician who made it and decorated with drawings by Katie and other talents and then by a friend; it became a prized possession for the kid who wore it.

The cast room went from blank white ceiling and walls to an entertainment center for kids on the cast tables. Model airplanes made by volunteers hung from the ceiling along with dirigibles and blimps and starships. The walls were decorated with pictures and cutouts of the residents in costumes from Roman gladiators to gorillas.

The whole room reflected Katie's warmth, knowledge, and concern for kids. The residents thought of their months under Katie's tutelage as an integral part of their training. This was an exposure that made them concerned human beings and physicians.

Katie became well known in the orthopaedic world and when the National Organization for Orthopaedic Nurses was formed, Katie became its president and formulated its educational program.

The hospital nursing administration had no real contact with the atmosphere that Katie had created in the clinic and cast room and no knowledge of the education that went on there. A supervisor was appointed for this area who had been a colonel in the U.S. Army Nursing Corps. She visited the cast room and was aghast at the flying teddy bears that hung from the wall. The supply closet was cleaned out and restacked with plaster rolls for casts that were cheaper and not suited for all uses. All this was done with no consultation with Katie or the physicians who worked there.

The physicians did not use the new supplies and had to borrow what they needed from other areas of the hospital. The pictures, the model airplanes, and the animals reappeared from an apparently inexhaustible supply as others were removed.

Katie, now discouraged, retired and lives in an apartment decorated with the mementoes that had made life in an orthopaedic work day an enjoyable learning experience. It also kept young patients wanting to see the room, the doctors, and Katie again.

Now the demand for quality has fallen before the economics of providing care. Good quality of care still has economic value, but other forces have entered the marketplace to threaten it.

Chapter III
Medical Practice Today

Criteria for the Insurance Company's Choice of Physician

The insurance company now selects its care providers on the basis of how little they have to pay to get the services. This also shuts the door on free choice of physicians for the patient. The insurance company can only allow you to go to a physician who has subscribed to an agreed-upon price for services. Physicians know that there are talented individuals among them and those with lesser talents and that the obtaining of superior skills may be an important adjunct to the survival of a patient with a life-threatening condition. The insurance companies have been forced to subscribe to a philosophy that insists that the physician be known as a particular type of purveyor, radiologist, internist, orthopaedic surgeon, genito-urinary surgeon, hematologist, etc., in order to fill a slot in the care panel. After that, price is the most important consideration. There is a progressive move to the fringes of less quality in order to achieve viable economics for the seller of the health care contract.

There is another important way to drive the care-quality standards downward. This is the substitution of a lesser level of care for a high level. A nurse practitioner can be substituted for a doctor, a nurse's aide for a nurse, a technician for a nurse's aide. These individuals are providing care but not at the proficiency or skill level and safety as formerly.

An important principle of good medical care has assumed lesser importance. This involves making the diagnosis first in order to determine appropriate treatment. There is great waste of time and money in going down the path of repetitious inappropriate treatment only to discover what is the cause of the patient's complaint months later.

Don't Diagnose; Just Treat Symptoms: A Recipe for Disaster

There has been a major development in medical care to avoid making a diagnosis first. Treating pain rather than investigating its cause may be cheaper but shortcuts the diagnostic process essential to good care. This results in treatment specialists who render care on the basis of symptomatic complaints. Pain clinics are now common. HMOs allegedly maintain health care services to ensure that you will not become ill, but there never has been any proof that this is indeed an efficient course to follow. You can go to hypnotists, chiropractors, or purveyors of magic rays without ever learning what disease is causing your difficulty.

Avoiding diagnosis altogether is a poor way to start treatment. It leads to delays in getting appropriate treatment or endless expenses in providing useless treatment. This is shown in a treatment specialty such as physiotherapy. There is a massive political push by the physiotherapy groups to do away with the doctor's prescriptions. The doctor presumably has recognized what is wrong with the patient and needs the physiotherapist's help to overcome the disability. In other words, the patient has gone through a diagnostic process before treatment began; without diagnosis the treatment may be inappropriate. Common sense would support the thesis that the treatment should be appropriate and aimed at improving the patient's condition.

We have developed enormous rehabilitation programs in this country. Rehabilitation is thought of as good for you. As the chairman of the first medical advisory committee of what has become a massive rehabilitation center and is now a beautiful facility in western Pennsylvania, I observed some tendencies as the program grew that led to corruption of the fundamental values of applying rehabilitation techniques. It is important to make a diagnosis and render definitive treatment prior to rehabilitation.

If diagnosis was not accurate before the patient entered the rehabilitation program, a disaster could ensue. This became more common as the word "rehabilitation" became a catchword for "cure." I remember a doctor's brother who was sent for rehabilitation only to discover after three months that his condition had progressed and his neurologic signs had become more evident. It became evident that he had a brain tumor. He had not had a diagnostic neurologic examination before entering rehabilitation.

A not uncommon problem was the extensive physiotherapy given to an individual who could not bear weight on his leg. Eventually the need for diagnosis prevailed and the disunited bone was diagnosed. Treatment would then be given by surgery for the nonunion before the patient entered the final phase of recovery. Once the bone was united, the function of the limb could be improved. This is fundamental to the practice of medicine and to procuring a cure.

Medical Care Today

In managed-care plans medical care is now thought to be less costly if symptomatic measures can satisfy the patient's demand for relief. The patient is led to less costly, but repetitious treatment, which is a step backward from the important principle that diagnosis is an important preliminary to the onset of treatment.

In Minneapolis, a city where care is dominated by HMOs, the conclusion has been reached that loyalty to a favorite physician has a dollar value for the patient that isn't as high as previously thought. A dollar value has been assigned of $6, although just how this conclusion was reached is not clear. The maintenance of choice and the value of doctor-patient relationships are taking a backseat in managed-care planning. The value of choice is not evident to patients who are well and only becomes evident to those who are sick.

In medical-care planning the primary care physician is expected to do it all. Disincentives are in place to diminish referral to someone who should more accurately recognize the patient's condition. The less laboratory information that is used the higher the monetary reward for the physician, although the patient may have lost an important benefit.

The entire range of medical care problems is expected to be handled by the general practitioner, internist, gynecologist, or pediatrician. These primary care providers will readily admit to lack of experience and training in handling many illnesses encompassed in this approach. The contact for medical help continues with the substitution of the nurse or technician at the other end of the line where formerly the patient saw a physician. The interposition of this phone call between the patient's opportunity to see the physician presses the patient back into a prescription for symptomatic relief. This stance often leaves the patient with a lack of resolution or satisfaction that the problem has been taken care of.

Health care planners predict that administrative costs in the practice of medicine will be reduced from 22 percent of the patient's health care dollar to 12 to 14 percent by these changes.

For the first time nurses are in oversupply. Jobs are disappearing and many nurses cannot find work. Hospitals are laying off employees at all levels. Those that remain employed are being asked to expand their coverage, which means less individual attention for the patient.

The nurse coordinator is being asked to cover more than one unit. This means safety checks become more superficial and swift. The patient has lost some protection and the bedpan brigade is spread thinner. The helpers that do this work check your condition, not the nurse who is now seldom seen. For a minimal-care problem, this may suffice.

The patient can appreciate how uncomfortable and risky this situation can become when there are tubes in every orifice. The medication injected into the miles of tubing must be accurate in amount and content. Reactions to them must be instantly recognized. An untrained technician cannot be expected to recognize any problems, like a limb strapped in an uncomfortable position or a malfunctioning tube.

As nurses become scarce, so do their helpers; meanwhile, their job range is increased so their response time is lengthened.

The Nursing Profession

Many nurses find themselves placed in a position where

they must make independent medical decisions. They are used more and more as substitutes for the physician; some actively seek accreditation as independent practitioners. Many state legislatures are now being asked to legitimize this expanded role.

With lack of knowledge mistakes begin to increase. Lack of knowledge may carry with it the loss of ability to recognize a deteriorating condition. The solution needs the attention of someone with more experience and training. Diagnostic procedures often demand competent experts, well trained in performing and interpreting these methods.

Routine tasks may be contained satisfactorily by the nurse. Unfortunately, taking care of the sick is filled with unexpected surprises, which demand still more training. The more accurate the diagnosis, the safer and more successful the therapy becomes. This is why the use of nurses, therapists, and technicians grew up under the supervision of the physician. More efficient management procedures cannot do away with these safeguards without placing the patient at risk. Florence Nightingale, one of the founders of the nursing profession, recognized the need for more enlightened bedside care. The physician remained the leader of the team, who prescribed the measures to be taken.

Consider the visit to the dentist. The dental assistant cleans your teeth, notes situations that should be checked, and assists the dentist in doing a procedure. The assistant becomes very familiar with these situations, but this does not suggest that the assistant can do it all. The procedure has to fit the dental pathology to be successful. When found, the pathology may need to be treated on the spot with a regime that fits the now accurately-recognized condition. The dental assistant does not attempt to develop an independent practice.

The gatekeeper concept does not merely embody the use

of the general physical for the specialist but must define the use of the nurse as the first line of defense. It cannot be used to keep the patient from medical care. When is a respiratory illness a life-threatening one? This is a difficult-enough decision for a pediatrician to make; imagine how hard it is for a nurse. An important aspect of managed care is to keep the patient from using the physician, such as the specialist, unnecessarily. It is an important step for the patient's welfare that the skill necessary to accurately recognize and triage the condition be available at the onset of treatment.

Managed care does not include a clear definition of who does what job. As a patient, do you know whether those people in crisply starched whites are nurses, nurse's aides, assistants, or housekeeping help? Is the phlebotomy technician a nurse, physicians' assistant, technician, medical student picking up tuition money, or someone in white who has been shown how to draw blood? Is the physician an M.D., an osteopath, a chiropractor, a podiatrist, or someone masquerading as a physician? The waters are getting muddy with the goal to save money in the patient's care.

A Sample Patient Progression Today: Will Green's Story

Will Green is now seventy years old. In 1943 he was in the Naval Air Cadet program and its leading cadet as his company took the crash course in navigation at the University of North Carolina. As company commander he visited sick bay to see his friend. The friend, a former football player, had just had a meniscectomy by a Dr. Robinson. There was a one-inch incision over the joint line at the front of the medical side of his knee. The cartilage had been removed without inflaming the knee. There was no swelling and his friend could flex the knee ninety degrees without discomfort. As Will bent over to admire the incision his own knee buckled and he crashed to the floor. He awoke to find himself in the bed next to his friend. Dr. Robinson examined the knee and appreciated the fact that Will Green had torn a cartilage. Dr. Robinson said he could use the same small incision for Will if he wished to undergo therapy.

That afternoon Dr. Robinson was assigned to sea duty. His replacement, who arrived the next morning, was a neurosurgeon. He said that they could do the same operation the following day. Will found out later from the corpsman attached to his unit that the neurosurgeon went over to the morgue at the local medical school and did the operation on a cadaver, practicing for Will.

When Will examined his knee a few days after the operation, he found a six-inch-long incision on the inside of his knee and gross swelling and blood oozing from the incision when he attempted to bend the knee. His football-playing friend had already rejoined his unit and was on full duty. Will wanted to continue his career opportunity. His corpsman said he could issue orders to send Will out with the next group. So Will, with a swollen knee and cane in hand, left with the next group after getting the forwarding orders. The cane had to be thrown away and somehow he managed to climb into the airplane and press the control pedals firmly enough. The knee gradually quieted down.

Will had had a great track career in college and continued to run for exercise during his business career. The knee performed well. The years went by and Will retired, but he continued running and walking until he noted the development of severe pain at the joint line underneath his incision.

Will was now covered by his company's HMO contract. He contacted the secretary of this facility and stated that he would like to see an orthopaedic surgeon. The secretary was very nice but informed him that it would be necessary to see their primary physician first in order to have his knee evaluated and to determine what should be the appropriate course from that point.

Will dutifully showed up for his examination, which consisted of an evaluation of his general medical condition. The doctor who saw him told him that he would receive a card noting any deviations from the norm. After asking Will if he had any shortness of breath, he was told that nothing of interest was noted. The blood pressure was taken and he was asked if he had any complaints. Will spoke of the pain in his knee. He was lying on his back on the examining table and the doctor flexed his knee and extended his hip. He was told that the motion was good. When Will persisted in his complaint, the doctor said that an MRI examination would be taken to see if there was anything abnormal.

Will, unsatisfied, decided to go outside the system at his own expense. The MRI was a $1,000 test, which the HMO would underwrite. Will wanted someone to look at the apparent source of his complaint. He did not want to give up his exercise routine if he did not have to.

Will went to a friend, an orthopaedic surgeon. The first order of the day was listening to Will tell the fifty-year-old story of his knee complaint. His history as a runner and track star and the meniscectomy was reviewed. Will stood in his undershorts so that his weight-bearing stance could be appreciated. The orthopaedic surgeon asked if Will had noted that he had developed some bowing at the knee that had undergone the meniscectomy.

With the patient lying on his back, the surgeon examined Will's hip and noted that internal rotation at both hips was limited. The knee was stressed to open it medially by carrying the ankle laterally. A jog of motion as the knee opened laterally was apparent to Will.

When the knee was palpated, there was found to be tenderness along the medial joint line. Beneath the scar a palpable mass of tissue was found at the joint line, which was actually tender. With flexion and extension of the knee, no roughness was appreciated. The knee cap was moved from side to side and was not painful.

The ankle was not swollen and when stressed was stable. There was no edema of the lower leg when the doctor's examining finger indented the tissues.

The patient and his doctor then sat down together to discuss what had been found. The doctor told Will that the history of meniscectomy long ago was relevant. The bowing of his leg also supported the fact that narrowing of the compartment of the knee had developed. This was consistent with traumatic arthritis of the medial or inside compartment of the knee. The tenderness that Will had at the joint line beneath the incision supported the diagnosis. Will had undergone a history and physical in order to arrive at a diagnosis of medial compartment arthritis due to trauma.

What was necessary to confirm these observations was what Will needed: a weight-bearing X ray of his knee. This should show narrowing of the joint on the inside with weight bearing. An MRI was not as diagnostic as the simple weight-bearing X ray. When the X ray confirmed this finding, Will was faced with several choices.

The limitation of Will's activity beyond what he was willing to tolerate could determine what course he wanted to follow.

If the discomfort was not severe enough to prevent walking to stay in shape, he could use mild anti-inflammatory drugs on a regular basis to control the discomfort and continue with his exercise routine.

If Will's quality of life was endangered by his complaint, then surgical straightening of the leg below the knee could move the weight bearing to the lateral (outside) compartment of the knee, where he still had a good joint surface of healthy cartilage.

A careful history and physical examination determined what Will wanted to know. He was able to avoid an expensive test done by someone unfamiliar with the history of joint difficulties after meniscectomy.

The more we substitute administrative management for medical management, the more expensive and less satisfying (to the patient) is the process of seeking medical care and relief of symptoms. Not all disease is life threatening; much of ageing involves a decline in the quality of life. The patient only gets one chance to travel down life's path. Improving our quality of life at every stage is a desire that we all have.

The practice of medicine still involves listening, talking, touching, and examining. No matter what you hear of today's wonder machines for diagnosis, they cannot tell what to examine without someone putting down directions. After this process the examination often means the expensive test is no longer necessary. The fundamentals of good medicine have not changed.

The Gatekeeper Concept and the HMOs

Elaine, a member of the Social Service Department of a local hospital, had been seeing the same gynecologist for several years. The hospital's new carrier was Blue Cross Select Blue. The new insurance coverage took effect the day Elaine went to see her gynecologist for a previously recommended procedure. She was duly placed in stirrups on the treatment table. The gynecologist was seated and ready to begin her procedure.

"By the way, Elaine," she asked, "who is your insurance carrier?"

"It was just changed today to Blue Cross Select Blue," Elaine replied.

The gynecologist stopped her procedure. "We'll have to check with them to see if it's all right to go ahead," she said. There was a one-half-hour interval while the insurance company was called.

After lengthy discussions between the gynecologist's secretary and the gatekeeper's office the procedure was approved if she would bear 20 percent of the cost. Otherwise, she would have to get down and see the gatekeeper physician in order to get a referral for the procedure.

The practice of medicine in this way appears to involve much more time, effort, expense, and the hiring of additional individuals than the way medicine was formerly practiced. Good general practitioners, or generalists of whatever background, have difficulty with the gatekeeper concept. Physicians with high responsibility to the patient recognize the enormous factual knowledge necessary to practice medicine and the difficulty in having command of every situation. So much of what we are striving to do to our doctors is based on limiting their ability to help the patient solve the problem at hand. The generalist often feels the need for help when the situation is beyond his level of confidence. The insecurity limits the ability to support the patient's happiness factor as the patient is made to wander through medicine's maze to find someone who can solve and treat the problem.

The HMO approach rewards the gatekeeper who does not refer to specialist care. Many also have financial penalties for those who do seek help for their patient. If each referral carries a penalty charge deducted from the gatekeeper's paycheck, then the devotion to the patient's problem has been influenced beyond what good medical practice indicates should be done.

Big use is made of scanning procedures by the gatekeeper. This theoretically says everything has been examined. It is possible to deny care without leaving a trail that could be unearthed by an investigator. What is regularly tested for? Chemical values indicating disease? It costs little more to run twenty tests on one of today's automated chemical machines than it does to run the scan for twelve values. Thus we are scanned for abnormalities of liver or kidney function, diabetes, and heart disease.

This is small section of the afflictions that beset a patient trying to get through life with a chance to enjoy it. Doctors want to see their patients solve their problems. Since access of the patient to further care is severely limited, some of the physician's desire to serve is not rewarded by involvement in a successful solution for the patient. Extra hours of work do not benefit the patient. The end result is the shaping of the "nine-to-four" doctor. There are no telephone calls to reach this physician. If the patient feels an urgency in handling his symptoms, the phone call service will supply someone to talk to. This is often not a physician but a nurse, nurse practitioner, or a technician trained to handle the calls to a solution satisfactory to the patient.

If the patient must be seen in order to protect the wellbeing of the HMO as well as the patient, then there is an emergency setup response, but there is no physician familiar with the case to talk to. Anyone who has arrived at the emergency room in a hospital has discovered that the initial investigation involves what insurance card you carry, not what is your complaint. Emergency rooms are an expensive way to care for routine complaints.

The Annual Physical

The annual physical examination is a frequently touted perk to sell an HMO policy. Would it surprise you to find that there has never been any scientific evidence to show that an annual physical examination prevents disease?

You can make a case that someone who is overweight could benefit by being told so. Someone who is in heart failure could be led to treatment. Someone with a mass in the abdomen could be led to further examination. But to prevent disease? Only in the sense of reinforcing good health habits. Preventing the development of cancer? Highly questionable. Early recognition of serious disease? Only in the sense of scanning chemical values of the common variety. The physical examination that prevents disease has not yet been invented.

Referral

The administrators of HMOs feel they can save money by limiting referral to specialized care. When referral to a physician who could solve the problem was done, it was an efficient area in the old days where the diagnosis was made and treatment became accurate and specific. It will take a period of time to realize that this is the economic way to go and better for the health of the patient.

The generalist wanted to make you well in private practice days and was your physician and used good judgment. Decisions about more specialized services went through him. There was no financial penalty attached to referrals. Instead there was a realization that the efficient use of specialists saved money and time and emotional stress for the sick patient. The designers of medical care have imposed financial penalties to limit referral to specialized care. It follows that saving money becomes a guidepost for care. If you have to go on a waiting list to arrive two years later at the opportunity to get your hernia repaired, you have undergone the discomfort and worry and occasional complications that could occur in this waiting period. You, the patient, are not the primary object of the good offices of this plan.

How could this concept save money? The unauthorized use of services was limited by the gatekeeper's choice, not yours. One of the facts of medical practice is the desire of the patient to be reassured as a result of fear of a disease that has developed. There is a real demand from patients who have read or heard or seen a disease consequence that could distantly resemble a symptom or sign that they have. This is a concern that patients feel and need to have answered. For some, the generalist's explanation is all that is necessary. For others, concern goes deeper, and only the deliberations of a perceived expert and tests will assuage this fear.

Career Choice—Medicine Becomes Corporate Practice

One of the attractions in a medical career back when it occurred to me that I had to make a choice was the independence that it offered. I reviewed other professions. Engineers had spoken to me about how empty they felt their work was. There was no chance to feel that they were contributing to the welfare of their fellowman, which explains their willingness to use their off hours to design braces or aid in making joint implants successful. Nobody feels more wounded when a lawyer attacks them in court for the failure of an implant or the downing of a plane than the engineer. Lawyers have an opportunity for making an impact on society, but seldom is it done. Architects have my sympathy when they drag in the sixth set of drawings to the criticism of the committee. In medicine the physician was beholden to his conscience and the plight of his patient. It was possible to see and feel the influence for health and well-being that one could exert.

The clouds swirling around the practice of medicine are changing what medicine can do to alleviate human suffering. The stock market makes a point in this regard in the rising stock prices of health care companies. They drive the cost down with contracts because of their patient control of large groups. The cost of the contract they sell is competitive with other plans but includes a handsome profit.

Corporations Practicing Medicine

Managed care has been able to make contracts for drugs, hospital devices, and physician services at a diminished cost.

Corporations have become many-armed practitioners of medicine. The not-for-profit hospital has disappeared. The major ones are now profit-making ventures, while the smaller ones are being purchased by managed health care plans. All sorts of reasons are advanced to explain why these companies can change the unprofitable to profitable. If there is a cash flow, the expenses and the charges can be adjusted to show a profit.

When I first became aware of hospital accounting, I was amazed to find that no one knew the actual cost of supplies and services to the individual patient. I suggested to the Blue Cross board, of which I was a member, that we ought to be able to tell what it cost an individual hospital to do a given procedure and thus to compare the efficiency of one hospital to another. No one was enthralled with this concept, but I believe that Blue Cross in Connecticut attempted to put a similar idea into practice. There may have been too much resistance to get a clear-cut idea of its value.

The accounting done by hospitals was so minimal that they resorted to pricing based on what the traffic would bear. This resulted in the $5 aspirin tablet. The only determinant of cost was whatever it would take to balance the books.

With costs growing beyond the rate of inflation and with one-day charges going beyond the ability of anyone to pay them, we need to be more realistic. We ought to be able to learn what it actually costs a given hospital to house a patient for a given procedure for one day. A friend of mine received a bill for a one-day stay in the hospital cardiac intensive care unit of $53,000. Is this the actual cost? Which hospital is efficiently run and which isn't? Is the hospital with the largest profit the best managed hospital, or is it merely overcharging?

The Emergency Room

One culprit in the increase in hospital costs is the emergency room. When patients enter they may get a basic charge that is the same for a cold as it is for an accident victim with a ruptured spleen. Emergency rooms have sprung up in most institutions and in some more informal settings. There are two basic reasons for this: first, the physician is not as available as in former years; second, the patient seeks a one-stop access to all the medical equipment that might be needed. An important drawing card is the availability of parking space.

The cost for a visit to this heavily staffed entity could be better controlled if each patient did not get the full charge for the facility and its equipment. A simple ten-minute interview with a physician could determine what might be necessary before committing to a package. Anyone who has sought treatment in an emergency room has experienced an interview by a clerk at the registration desk. This may be the most extensive interview of the hospital visit, and not surprisingly, it puts the form of insurance that the patient carries ahead of what is wrong with him. When the bill is totalled up there is a readily-perceived discrepancy between what the patient received and the charge for the visit.

The emergency room is clearly not appropriate for the casual practice of family medicine, but no one wants to do anything about the phenomenon. The patient has been forced to turn to the emergency room because it is available. The changing attitudes of physicians, where high priority is placed on regulated hours, the increasing number of female practitioners who have other responsibilities such as family care have all combined to make the physician less available.

Some hospitals have recognized the inappropriateness of an emergency room visit for routine family care problems and maintain a less expensive family clinic as well as an emergency room. Patients are triaged and sent to the appropriate facility as they enter a common entrance. Physicians need to take more responsibility for the provision of care. Since they have experienced a divorce from the administration of a hospital's facilities this has become hard to do.

Emergency room physicians are a new breed of doctor who work an eight-hour shift until relieved by the next team. There is little on-going contact with the same physician in future visits and the patient often starts at square one on the next visit to explain their complaint. There are many physicians who seek this type of employment, often because of unrelated circumstances such as motherhood and child care.

Some emergency rooms really serve as family care facilities. Others function as a depository for the victims of violent street crimes. In this type there are often stretchers with patients in various types of severe distress, who are in long lines waiting to get into the operating room. In one type the emergency room has a brief flurry of activity from a family who has been waiting for Dad to get home from work. Dad is usually so famished he gets something to eat before he does his duty and takes the kid to the emergency room. After these family visits the emergency room becomes a quiet place, but must still maintain the staff of at least a clerk, a nurse, a physician, an X ray and laboratory technician. No hospital wants to shut down the emergency room since this jeopardizes their flow of patients who might pass their door to get to their competitor. As a result I have seen two fully staffed emergency rooms quietly passing the night within three hundred yards of each other.

Intensive Care Beds

The intensive care bed is the most expensive accommodation that the hospital can supply. If you have ever been in or visited such an area you know that each bed is a monitoring bed with oxygen-trained personnel and electro-cardiogram at the bedside. The scene is very labor-intensive.

Only the room in which a patient recovers from surgery comes as close to providing constant attention from the personnel and regular monitoring of the patient. If the bed is classed as being of the intensive care variety, the cost (charges) mounts into many thousands of dollars each day. There is an abundant opportunity for the hospital administration to make up for losses in other areas by using these beds. In one hospital that I am familiar with a great deal of transplant work is done. A patient awaiting a transplant is frequently very ill. While awaiting a suitable organ, he or she may be in a hospital in an intensive care bed. They are sick people but they have often been waiting at home. They may wait many weeks for a donor who may never appear. In the hospital their readiness to receive the transplant is constantly evaluated by the staff.

When Blue Cross or any other agency agrees to pay for transplants it takes on this cost. Of course it is ultimately you, the subscriber, who pays. The types of patients and the types of disease problem can markedly affect the profit that a hospital is able to make. When the contract that an insurance source has with a hospital is essentially a cost-plus arrangement for reimbursement, we are exposed to sky-rocketing costs.

The HMO

The HMO as a system of medical practice has received a mixed reaction from the public, patients, and physicians. There are large population groups covered by HMO plans, since the contracts are most frequently with corporations or organizations and cover their employees or members. The purchase of the contract has been made possible by the lower cost of health care coverage. This book defines the nature of the coverage on many avenues. The record of savings has been variable, generally less than that offered by other health care systems. The dissatisfaction level of the employees or members is low if the group is young, but rises as the group grows older and needs more care.

The HMO concept had an early success rate when it was used by an early managed-care plan in California. One of the features of the success rate was the young age of the employees that were covered. The physician employees of the plan were idealistic and treading on new ground—an incentive to make it work. The physicians were generally young and desirous of getting started in California. After contacts were established and the confidence level of the physicians rose, they tended to leave for a practice in which they were more in control of the patients and their own destiny.

Blue Cross has adopted the HMO concept where it suited it in its competition with other insurance companies. Blue Cross has left its founding concept of providing a means for patients seeking protection from medical bills that were associated with a major health crisis and serving as a repository and disbursing agent for a minimum administrative overhead of 5 percent. Blue Cross has become a profit-making corporation, utilizing its cost ties with hospitals to secure a favorable rate of reimbursement. It now seeks to influence medical-care values to enhance its profit-making possibilities. Blue Cross enters into public relations endeavors, advertising, and all forms of health care policies to cover the field.

Blue Cross utilizes its profit-making capabilities to provide perks for its executives and has been very successful in recruiting top-quality executives. Gifts to specific universities and medical centers are made with funds provided by those subscribers protecting themselves against medical expenses. As the Blue Cross plan enters into attempts to influence medical care organizations and determine who it will support and who it will not, it has become an ally of some hospitals and physicians. Since Blue Cross has enlarged its scope and objectives it would aid the development of a level playing field in the contest with other insurance companies if it no longer had a specific relationship with some hospital administrations who are making a profit without being asked to lower their per-diem rate. There is a frequent request of medical practitioners by the Blue Cross organization to lower their rates, but the relationship with hospitals resembles more closely a partnership in business together.

Chapter IV
Medicine for the Future

The Patient and the Doctor

Have you ever feared that you had to see the doctor and the desire to avoid the encounter was very real? It doesn't matter how old you are, the feeling is still the same. As a child you knew there was no place to hide. You knew that your mother felt like you did but must take you by the hand and go. You don't resent that; she has no place to hide either. Her wet hand would not let you go as she tried to communicate strength and sympathy to you.

When you are a young adult there is no doctor. The world will go on the same way every day and you will be able to do everything. There is no thought to interrupt that feeling. You don't even remember the doctor and the needles and the no-alternative approach. Even the kind look and the warmth of the arm on your shoulder didn't seem to help in those early days. In middle age you are free unless you are very unlucky because disease potential is less.

As you get older, reason begins to tell you that perhaps just a checkup now and then might be wise. After those episodes, when the doctor told you that you were in as good physical shape as anybody that had ever been examined, there was gratitude and relief. You even thought the doctor was as good a person as you had ever encountered. You were examined, you took the big risk, and you passed. What a good feeling! You had at least another year of the good life.

As you progressed into middle age, your friends were beginning to appear on hospital lists for operations. There were serious times for those you knew, and you wondered why it was not you. Now the occasional tests produced little warning signs. The prostate antigen test produced a little higher number. The blood pressure wasn't that of a young person any more. Physical limitations for what you always had regarded as an easily performed task began to appear. Your friends began to appear with early coronary artery attacks, diabetes, and strokes, often very minimal, but there nonetheless. Some friends now were diagnosed as having cancer.

Now going to the doctor was again a dreaded appointment. The result was unknown. You still wanted to find some place to hide but knew there was none. There was no one who took you by the hand because you had to go. You knew you had to go and that something you did not want to hear might be said. You hoped for kindness and understanding if there was an unexpected finding, and fortunately the kindness is usually there.

The individuals who were doctors that you depended on gave you an understanding of life and the odds that you faced. When you were faced with serious treatment and knew that you had to surrender your body and yourself to the care of someone else, your relationship to this person became very important. You needed someone at the bedside who made you feel warm, secure, and utterly relaxed. You gave someone else the responsibility for your body when you could.

If you did not have the confidence you might have had when you looked into the face of the doctor, you lost some of your ability to overcome the fear of the threat to your well-being. If you had the inner knowledge that everything would be done that could be done, you relaxed and passed the worry that you had to your doctor. It was a comforting feeling; you wanted to be sure that the person on whom you depended would be there tomorrow. Because you knew that if that person were there, you would walk out of that place.

A doctor who has your confidence means a lot to your ability to get well. As a patient you really don't want to denigrate that feeling. It means that later on you wonder why you were worried at all. There are little touches that communicate things left unsaid and big things that are met head on with someone there to help you.

You as a patient can't substitute a clinic and the atmosphere that does not know who you are for the feeling of being able to lean a little on someone else when you are in trouble with any unknowns.

We can't let all this go without noting how important it is to preserve good medical care. Society needs the security that comes with the knowledge that the person at the bedside knows about these things and will use that knowledge to help you. As a patient you can't let the relationship you have with your doctor be supplanted by a business that does not know about you.

When I was a surgical intern at Boston Children's Hospital, I was assigned as the physician to inject the only medicine we had to prevent the ravages of hemophilia. Unfortunately, the injection had to be given every day to maintain a normal clotting time. If there were repeated hemorrhages into joints, the disease would soon destroy them. The unexpected bleeding into vital organs could be life threatening.

Louis Diamond, the chief, was a kind man who specialized in hematology. The only tool in his hands at that time that would ameliorate the disease was the injection of human blood plasma. This was made from human blood from many individuals from which the red cells had been removed. The treatment was crude. There were complications in the process of delivering this exposure to blood plasma in such chronic amounts. Louis Diamond could not face the screaming children who came in daily for their injections. That job was passed down to the intern. I could hear these children screaming on the street outside the hospital as they approached the open window of the out-patient clinic. The mother was in as much distress as the child, but when both of them were in front of me, they were suddenly quiet. I had already prepared the materials for injection so that they did not have to watch.

It was over quickly and gratitude filled the room. I had developed the skill that comes with many repetitions and was the only security the patient had. I can still remember the screams from the street outside even though it was over forty years ago. Fortunately, the next year saw the development of blood fractionation and a more humane treatment that did not require daily injections. Progress in medicine is a wonderful thing.

Capitalism, Computers, and Kemeny

When John Kemeny was a leading mathematician and president of Dartmouth College, he frequently prodded the social sciences to add the logic of mathematics to their deliberations. Kemeny had written the first computer language (ABC) and was a pioneer in bringing computer use to each and every student. Economics lent itself most easily to the integration with mathematics, but sociology and political science were difficult social sciences to make precise. Kemeny's ability to put computer language into our daily life affected medical machinery as well.

One of the Dartmouth students in 1970 was Robert Reich, currently the secretary of labor in the Clinton cabinet. Reich espoused social equality by promoting the redistribution of wealth. This stance has some validity when wealth is held in indolent hands, but little validity when wealth is used to make major advances for society, new products, and scientific advances. Without wealth these changes do not occur and major industrial societies such as that of the United States do not occur. Products and jobs are not created and opportunity becomes a sometime thing.

Capitalism has spawned the development of major educational and research institutions in medicine. From these have come individuals trained in new techniques, researchers able to devise new products, and an uplift to the basic level at which medicine is practiced.

If we have planners, governmental or private, skimming off the top of the investment money, we are going to lose the opportunities open to our best students. The growth of health research institutions and the development of new medicines will falter. When wealth becomes the property of politicians through taxes, the dominant thought in the minds of these individuals becomes their survival. We lose entrepreneurship and originality. The growth of innovations such as the use of computers in medicine lacks sponsorship. Medicine developed tomograms (essentially slices on X-ray film) of segments of the human body through the skillful incorporation of the computer. We added the rapidly developing computer science and now had computerized tomography. As a result, we can now see inside the human body in three dimensions. We can stand as if we were inside a fractured and badly damaged pelvis. We can walk around these damaged structures and visualize how they should be put back together. The possibilities that we now have to reconstruct after trauma could not have been done ten to fifteen years ago. The machinery that we now have goes back to Kemeny's introduction of computer language into our thinking.

Transplants of the organs of those who have just died into the body of the living with a damaged part has a real limitation of supply that could and must result in choices of recipients being made. We can never expect to match the demand. The alternative is to provide the improvement of the part we have. In the heart we are into this approach already. We repair vessels to improve blood supply. We exercise muscle that has been damaged and thus improve the function of the cells that are left. We need to support the efforts of those trained individuals who are developing these new approaches. They come from many fields. If we develop a system that does not support future progress or new medication, we can stagnate the whole process. Venture capital is a necessary tool to make progress happen.

Nobody has been able to devise a system for human endeavors that can plan for the future accurately enough. The law of supply and demand and the growth of opportunity can do things for our society which elude the planners.

The threat to continuing progress in medicine is illustrated by two events that have occurred to influence a major medical center.

The HMOs have forced the reduction of the cost for transplant surgery so that it is reduced by half. What once cost $300,000 is now billed at $150,000. If HMOs are going to control the flow of patients, then they are going to send them to the least-cost center. It happens that the center where the know-how was developed to make transplant surgery a reality is also one of the most expensive. Patients are being denied access to this center on economic grounds. Can we keep up progress in medicine under these circumstances?

In my old orthopaedic clinic the patients are now seen by a chiropractor and a physiotherapist. The reason that drives organized medicine to do this is economic. Health insurance will pay for a visit in the clinic to a chiropractor or physiotherapist, but not to specialty care by an orthopaedist unless there is a bureaucratic license.

How Socialized Medicine Spawns Private Health Care Insurance

Would it surprise you to know that one of the great growth industries in Great Britain and in New Zealand where governmental control of medicine first appeared is private health insurance? It has become a phenomenon because socialized medicine has not answered the demand for care of the general public.

In England if you are relegated to a waiting list for the surgical correction of your hernia, years may go by without a call to come in for care. The facilities are not adequate and new hospital construction has fallen off compared to the population growth and has not approached the rate that existed prior to socialized medicine. If you have enough discomfort and grow impatient with the waiting list that you find yourself a part of, then you are going to seek alternatives.

Since this involves an additional expense, there is a growing demand for health insurance to make the underwriting of this private care a possibility. For the middle-income group the demand is high so that it can become possible to speed up the delivery of desired care and to obviate the rationing aspect of governmental underwriting. In Britain the massive hospitals of bygone years are now part of a system run by the governmental bureaucracy.

The alternative site in England to provide care underwritten by health insurance or private funds is the conversion of a row of brownstones into a medical facility. This conversion obviously cannot approach the equipment and personnel of a major hospital. The brownstones provide an efficient mode of care transmission and are responsive to the physicians' needs in the care of their patients.

Robert Reich might have seen in his stay at Oxford as a Rhodes scholar the need to contain and control the population to put the group into lockstep with the governmental plan. A punitive provision was a part of an early version of one government's health care plan. It was there to block those who would try to get around the system. Private underwriting and endowment helped in the Nuffield Orthopaedic Center in Oxford, which operated at a level of care beyond the standard set by government. Robert Duthie headed this center, which drew trainees and visitors from the Commonwealth and the United States.

Some of Duthie's career had been spent at Strong Memorial and the University of Rochester Medical School. He knew what outstanding personnel and equipment existed in the world and spent a good portion of his working time raising funds to make sure it was supplied at the Nuffield.

The administrators running the governmental bureaucracy and controlling socialized medicine in England did not hesitate to use the private funds to supplant and make unnecessary the use of government funds to provide the equipment and services.

One major step forward for British medicine was made possible when a donor gave funds for the purchase of a modern diagnostic machine or facility. By contrast, such steps were scarce in the socialist plan for the total welfare. That such outlays led to a higher level of excellence was not a valid reason for doing them, in the minds of bureaucrats.

Under governmental control these donors became less

and less numerous. These improvements could only be made in the broad plan when the need became overwhelming and for a particular area. It was only possible in competition with the needs of the rest of the population—and only by winning the approval of the administrators for the district.

Extraordinary Medical Efforts Arise to Combat Dictatorships

The advances of medical care can be prevented in other ways. Hitler, for instance, had little interest in promoting health facilities for his constituents. As a result, Germany fell from its position as a leader in medical advances and facilities before World War I into a state bereft of this type of civilized advance after World War II. A dictatorship is of little help when its aims do not include a means of keeping the population well.

In World War II it was impossible for a German hospital to maintain even the supply of enema bags and nozzles for an elementary human need. The German surgeons were acutely aware of this. Even so, an interesting advance was spawned by human ingenuity and a caring attitude.

In World War II British aviators were eventually returned to England in a prisoner exchange program. Some of these victims of air crashes were believed, upon repatriation, to have been victims of a despicable human experiment. They were found in England to be walking on previously fractured femurs. Inserted in the femur was a long metal rod which was visible on X-ray film. The hue and cry on this discovery was enormous. It was another example of German brutality in the minds of many.

Eventually the truth became known. These individuals were fortunate enough to have been cared for by disciples of

Professor Boehler of Vienna. Hitler had decreed the death sentence for any patient not discharged from the hospital in one month. Under previous treatment regimes this was an impossibility for individuals with a fractured femur, who were subjected to months of traction immobilization followed by a hip cast that immobilized the leg.

Boehler, with his humanitarian instincts, found a way to get these individuals discharged from the hospital in one month. He devised a rod inserted from hip to knee to support the fractured femur. The technique and the materials and the design used today are a considerable improvement. Nonetheless, these primitive devices worked on a grand scale. These individuals were discharged, walking, in less than one month.

Some were British aviators who were returned to England and were able to fly in combat once again. The initial reaction was overcome by orthopaedic surgeons who recognized the major advance spawned by a stressful situation. A dictatorship may not be the answer to improved medical care. Blind edicts stimulate clever solutions to get around them. Boehler, far from being an inhumane experimenter, was eventually shown to be the savior of lives and the father of a major medical advance.

Germany, depleted of medical resources in people and ideas by Hitler, has spent the ensuing decades catching up. The stress of some situations sponsors heroic efforts, but there must be idealistic and sympathetic physicians to bring these advances to reality. German medicine contributed a major advance, even in the face of being destroyed.

Society Needs Scientists

I was impressed during the later years in the 1950s by the arrival in my department of an athletic, piano-playing, cigarette-smoking, handsome German orthopaedic surgeon named Gerhard Enders from Stuttgart, Germany. After a brief period in my training program, Gerhard asked if he could bring a young woman from Germany to work at the University of Pittsburgh. She was a virologist, and I found a job for her in the laboratory of Jonas Salk, who was busy growing the polio virus in order to make the polio vaccine.

She was one of the most attractive young individuals that I have ever encountered. Her name was Gisela Enders and she and Gerhard had an apartment in the medical school area (not the most desirable). She was very intelligent, and while Jonas Salk was working on the polio vaccine, she developed the vaccine for measles. I doubt if Jonas had had many individuals this talented working in his laboratory. She now heads an institute of virology in a city near Stuttgart. Hitler almost destroyed Germany, but individuals such as Gisela and Gerhard Enders have brought it back. Individuals can make a difference in the practice of medicine.

A Science Needs a Humanitarian to Render Maximum Service to Society

Bill Berenberg was a pediatrician who bridged the gap between the clinicians and the scientists at Harvard Medical School. What Bill saw with the thick glasses he wore was your emotions and your reactions; not many could see so well.

This led Bill to take over the cerebral palsy clinic at Boston Children's. I was the young orthopaedic surgeon for this group and was followed by Henry Banks, who brought his organizational skills to the care of these children. Henry's administrative skills were recognized when he became the dean of medicine at Tufts University in Boston in 1990.

The encounter with Bill Berenberg and a charming personality at Boston Children's named Sidney Farber, a silver-tongued orator and pathologist, led to the largest single gift Harvard Medical School has ever received. This consisted of $50 million to underwrite a massive attack to improve the understanding and care of cerebral palsy. The donor was Leonard Goldenson.

Excellence in medicine is not the sole province of physicians. It grows when insightful individuals in society recognize the need to advance and are able to do something about it. This becomes a less attractive area when it becomes the province of administration, whether government-supported or institution-supported. The amazing thing about the human race is the number of individuals who want something better and are willing to devote themselves to doing something about it. The individuals who want something better are seldom the planners who themselves are not directly involved in how the system works. Their thinking is rather to recognize what in their minds is the greatest good for the greatest number. We tend to be reduced to a faceless, muddy mass by this type of planning. It is seldom possible for a gifted individual to make his presence felt in this system. The deficiencies are not recognized, and the ability to correct them is smothered. Nonetheless, people will find a way, and this is occurring despite the fact that a government bureaucracy may be given control of medical care. Where the smothering occurs, medical institutions are in the decision-making hands of administrators who are not directly affected. Our society needs both patients and physicians influencing the growth and excellence of our medical care to keep on the ascending path. This explains the growth of private health insurance in the face of bureaucracy or administration. It helps to explain the penalties that are written into the form of the system desired by planners. Individuals must be able to circumvent the imposed system. It is more important that we continue to improve than that we make the plan survive without molestation.

A Poor State Improves Its Medical Care

New Hampshire is one of our poorest states in terms of job opportunities, but certain teaching institutions have been remarkably successful at providing work. In New Hampshire there are occasional successful economic enterprises such as L'EGGS stockings. This is a merchandising success derived from making plastic eggs to contain the product and display it. This is hardly a momentous advance for our civilization but it has provided work and a new life for old factories along the Merrimac River. These successes are few.

Individual intellectual pursuits provide an income for some. The lumber industry flourishes in New Hampshire, and this industry's income is supplemented by arts and crafts and hard-scrabble farms. The ski industry is very weather-dependent and occasionally has some good years.

There were not sufficient resources to improve medical facilities, so doctors did what they could on their own. In this area general practitioners were widely scattered, and many smaller towns did not contain such an individual. Ralph Miller was concerned about the level of care in the state, and as professor of pathology at Dartmouth Medical School, he had an idea to improve the level of excellence. The postmortem examination was an important tool to check the accuracy of diagnosis, but there were not pathologists in every area to carry out these Monday morning quarterbacking jobs. In order to remedy this situation, Ralph Miller spread himself thin and made himself available to many communities in New Hampshire. The only feasible way to avoid spending the working hours of every day on the road was to fly. So he became a pilot. He and his assistant increased the number of postmortem examinations in the state in remote areas and heightened the medical awareness of the practicing physicians. This was a single man's contribution to the welfare of many and improved the care for many individuals.

Ralph Miller died in a plane that he was piloting on a snowy night in New Hampshire; a mountain stood in his way. In the meantime, however, the number of physicians and the facilities they could use have grown to acceptable proportions, and Dartmouth has developed as the North Country Medical Center where specialist care is available.

Managed Care Is, First, a Business

It is apparent that managed care can interfere with care modalities that medicine has developed. One area that might impact heavily on you, the patient, if you are unfortunate enough to suffer severe injury, is the handling of patients who are brought to trauma centers.

These trauma centers have developed to answer a need. Not every hospital emergency room can handle severe motorcycle injuries that arrive on the doorstep. Trauma centers have been carefully graded and equipped with facilities and personnel. After severe multiple injuries, the patient is rapidly transferred to those centers where ability to handle the problem is available. Interference with this organization of medical facilities for ability to handle major disasters to the patient can occur when managed care steps in. Cost now becomes a major consideration, and approval for care and the use of these trained surgeons may not be given by the managed-care organization. At minimum, the care is complicated by paper and telephone work to secure approval from the underwriter each step of the way. Where speed in getting emergency care is essential, this may become a life-threatening situation.

The natural economic guideline for the traumatized patient is for the managed-care organization to secure transfer to its own organizational care facility as quickly as possible. New emergency-care coverage laws were passed in California to safeguard the patient when the decision to transfer may be demanded by the plan's administrations. As a patient you need the protection of medical judgment. Where transfer to a top-flight trauma center is delayed, then medical hazards arise to threaten the patient.

A case I am familiar with, as an example, was brought to a small hospital's emergency room, which was not able to adequately care for a severely traumatized patient in the middle of the night when personnel was limited to a nurse and technician. The result was inadequate replacement of fluid and blood loss. A single intravenous line could not keep up with the patient's needs during a several-hour ambulance run to a major center.

With blood volume down, the heart and lungs were not adequately exposed to oxygen, and the oxygen content of the blood fell to dangerous levels. This is a precursor to a severe complication that has been labeled "fat embolism syndrome." The efficiency of heart and lung function is not able to clear the accumulation of fatty acids from the lungs. As a result, tissue damage results, destroying lung tissue. In some cases the damage is beyond repair when the patient arrives at the center. Massive blood replacement then does not reverse the condition. Administrative governance of this transfer is not guided by medical guidelines but by managed-care administrative decisions unless we protect ourselves. We can be at the mercy of managed-care officials when this coverage rules the care of the patient. Although the contrast is more dramatic when speed of care is essential, this management can affect the patient's welfare in less urgent situations.

If every effort is being made to avoid specialist referral outside the plan, the waiting period for definitive care can lengthen into months and years. If the reward to the gatekeeper is present only when the patient is kept in the hands of managed-care personnel and a penalty to the gatekeeper ensues with referral outside the plan to a more appropriate physician or facility, the patient can suffer needlessly.

Women Find Their Place in Medicine

An important change that has occurred in medical care is the increasing number of women who are delivering the care. This has nothing to do with their ability, but rather their availability. The practice of medicine was changing even before managed-care and socialized-medicine proposals began reaching the public. The entrance of women into medical school and medical practice has markedly increased. This move has maintained the quality of the physician, and women are accepted as being equally skilled in a profession that was formerly predominantly male.

Female physicians, by nature of the demands to which their lives are subject, have had to make some compromises in the way they practice medicine. The division occurs primarily when the demands of family life put a handicap on the availability of women to practice medicine.

It is hard to raise children if work hours are not regular and dependable. Women have chosen fields in which patient demand can be scheduled with dependability. The prime fields that have this characteristic are roentgenology, anesthesia, emergency medicine, dermatology, and pathology. Work in these areas can be scheduled, and the time limits of involvement can be regulated. The person hired to substitute in the child-care area can be relieved with a predictable time schedule. What these female doctors do not receive from medicine is identity with the life and times of a particular patient. This is troublesome for many but accepted as a compromise in order to carry out a full routine in life.

This is a different experience than female physicians had had in the past when Connie Gyon was a well-known internist at Cornell Medical Center, New York Hospital. Connie answered the demand for a family physician for many prominent New Yorkers in the 1930s. She was an attractive, attentive, and intelligent physician, and for executives with heartburn from a troublesome ulcer she was a godsend. My grandfather was the dean at Cornell in those days so that we knew her well on the same basis as an accepted family member. Connie Gyon remained single throughout her life.

Connie interfaced with New Yorkers, and her popularity was reflected in the regard that executives had for her. Her whole life involved the care of these people. She served on the boards of some foundations when she was not serving as the physician to these board members. There was no need nor time to substitute other interests. I called her once in the 1950s to see if one of the foundations of which she was a board member would be interested in supporting me in an attempt to bring programmed education to medicine. She immediately knew who I was, but firmly told me that programmed instruction was not one of the fields that her foundation was interested in.

Another favorite female doctor of mine when I was in practice in Boston was Eleanor Howard. She had no children and headed the Anesthesia Department at Boston University's Medical School and Hospital in the 1940s and 1950s. She was married to Louis Howard, a professor of orthopaedic surgery. Eleanor Howard was able to devote her life to her patients, her teaching, and her committees. She was a striking, tall woman who was popular in all avenues of her career, a successful and loved physician.

Women in medicine prior to the 1960s had successful careers. They were less numerous than in today's world. Now that women are more numerous, a secondary aspect has been to increase the need of programmed modalities of care, which can operate on a scheduled basis.

Trustees and Research

I watched the change in medicine's control of its destiny with a minimal awareness of what was happening and in the beginning very little understanding.

My early contact with the trustees of the hospitals where I worked was filled with personal awareness of who we each were. I was sure the trustees were aware of the work we were doing and that they were interested in making sure that we had the tools to do it because their committee came by every few months without the administration. Chief Wilson, the CEO of ALCOA, was their chairman and always there. Trustees today could use the insight that existed in the 1950s and the 1960s when they personally knew who worked in an institution. They wanted outstanding individuals so that they could see the institution fulfill its function for the community. These trustees knew more about the hospital than the balance sheet. They resembled those individuals known as "trustees" in Boston, who have been responsible for the excellence of their institutions.

I began to notice that we weren't meeting with the trustees regarding the future planning for the institutional program and physical plant of the hospital, and then the personal visits by the trustees to my workplace stopped. I began to wonder how the trustees knew what was going on in their institutions. When you are busy, as they are, with many responsibilities, it is soporific to find the state of the hospital totally encompassed by the administrators' report and the financial state secure according to the balance sheet.

It doesn't leave much room for the trustees' input, which I assume is part of the grand design of a successful administration. As a member of the boards of some institutions with some responsibility in the world, I began to realize how cleverly I had been isolated from the working of the institution. The administration's ploy was to get a pigeon to run the meeting and obviate any serious discussion. But you always have to make sure you have lined up the pigeon first.

The underlying plan is to enlarge the budget but always make sure that you have a fund source ready to balance it. In the case of hospitals, the major fund source was, and is, patient activity, always being sure that it is underwritten by insurance. Insurance protects the wealthy from being inordinately charged to cover losses elsewhere. The wealthy make sure they are insured as well, being prudent people.

Funding From NIH

The teaching institutions also garner a significant income from research grants. The greatest source is the National Institutes of Health (NIH). In prior times research bled medical schools and associated hospitals to an anemic whiteness. The more research money that came in, the greater the liability to provide housing, laboratory equipment and personnel. It became a load that quickly put a lid on the ability to do research. It was unfair and economically impossible for private institutions to underwrite government research. The answer was to calculate the overhead associated with the activity generated by the research grant and add this percentage to the grant's total.

There has to be a meeting of minds that specifies what is admissible as overhead. Overhead rose from 10 to 50 percent once these floodgates were open. A percentage of the dean's and other administrators' salaries was put into this charge, as was a percent of the car pool, the heating plant, maintenance of the building, and all the people who kept the doors open. There were abuses, but these gradually became less challenging with the help of government auditors.

We do have healthy research support that is derived from government funds and are a fortunate nation in the world because the size of this support surpasses the the effort of any other nation. It requires an enlightened population, willing to have a portion of their taxes used to support research.

Funding of the National Institutes of Health as an institution and the grant program that supports research at many universities is subject to political influence. When the funding of research for AIDS passed the total for cancer or heart disease, this political influence was apparent.

AIDS may have been a genital disease of sheep in Uganda, but through mutations of the virus it has become a human scourge. It is not a pretty story, but further mutations in this disease can be expected in future years. Given man's behavior as a purveyor of sexual disease, our research may have a hard time keeping up with this virus.

The cost in the medical care that this one disease necessitates could be overwhelming. Society is being taxed for this cost but has no representation to control the behavior that spreads it. There are many medical problems increasing the cost of medicine, but this one is rapidly surpassing all others.

The time for the hue and cry against this cost is not apparent while it is being given, but when the cost must be paid. Somehow we are going to have to prepay our anticipated medical care costs.

The projected cost of medical care underwritten by the government has always been underestimated. The Medicare program has a cost that points this out. Yet when it was proposed, no one stepped forward and with reasonable honesty predicted the cost and its continued escalation. If this had been done, it might well have delayed the arrival of this government program. We stumble onward consistently oblivious to reality in medical care costs and always pointing the finger at someone else.

Chapter V
Trying to Find the Answer

Institutional Overhead

The past ten to fifteen years have seen a change in the character of medical schools and university-affiliated hospitals. In former times these institutions were the solid rock of medicine. The goal was to develop and support the high road of medical practice. It started with well-trained individuals who could do the skill part of medical practice better than others. They could also teach others. Their financial compensation was frequently less than their colleagues in the solo practice of medicine. The demands on the time of the teachers in medicine included the bedside and office practice, but also a full teaching schedule and the publishing of papers and books that reflected their clinical and laboratory research. There were invitations to talk and teach at meetings and other institutions, which meant travel and time away from a home practice and time at home. The university or hospital usually took an overhead charge from the practice income of the physician to support the expenses of teaching.

Some institutions were punitive in their tax on the full-time physicians so that it took a truly dedicated individual to pursue this course. The University of Chicago Medical School paid its full-time professors at a level consistent with the pay schedule of the liberal arts faculty. This was not in keeping with the financial rewards that had been experienced by the two outstanding practitioners and teachers who started the full-time system at the University of Chicago. Walter Palmer was eagerly sought by the wealthy of Chicago as their internist and guardian medical mentor. Dr. Palmer was highly rewarded in his income from private practice among this group of patients. His partner, as chief of surgery and originator of this practice plan, was a famous surgeon in Chicago, Dallas B. Phemister. Although a general surgeon, Phemister found himself drawn to the field of orthopaedics, where he made many contributions to the care of patients suffering from loss of blood supply or aseptic necrosis of the hip. He was a student of bone pathology as well, which influenced how the Orthopaedic Department at this university developed.

The chairman of the Orthopaedic Department was Howard Hatcher, who spent many of his teaching hours at a long table with many microscopes and chairs for the students. His enjoyment of life was heightened by their discussion of the slides of the pathology that they looked at together. The hospital and medical school where the department was lodged found its income challenged by an excessive charge for cleaning the windows. (There are many ways to overcome the antagonism that exists to taxation.)

Howard Hatcher was happy with his continuing study of bone pathology and it never occurred to him that he was being taken advantage of. His life was fulfilled by the intelligent orthopaedic surgeons that he trained, who carried his name far and wide.

When Dr. Hatcher retired, his former residents and students raised a fund to purchase a car for him. He had never been able to afford one. One might think that starting to drive late in life could lead to disasters. Fortunately this did not occur.

The Need for Institutional Support

The university and hospital have outgrown the support that a minor attention to the practice of medicine could provide. After all, there was a point where the final income to the physician was so low relative to other opportunities that it became hard to hire the good ones coming on-line in a new era. Now there is a further hazard to financial security for the teaching institutions as insurance companies' plans search for outlying hospitals with lower per-diem rates in which to put their plan members when they have to be hospitalized. For some of the plans this has meant purchasing the outlying hospitals and controlling their costs. After all, these managed-care plans are the product of corporations who exist when they are successful because of the profit that they can make from medical practice.

The knee-jerk reaction for the teaching institutions has been to meet this challenge head-on. This means forming a medical care plan often called an HMO and purchasing outlying hospitals themselves. The next step is the enlargement of the outpatient phase of their business. This means purchasing clinic and real estate and building outlying medical practice sites in order to draw patients into their orbit.

An approach that is occasionally taken reminds one of the gangster approach to competing businesses. Practitioners in the suburbs have been approached by the heads of a program at the university with an either/or proposition. The practicing physician is asked to send his surgical cases to the institution or they will build a practicing clinic next door and draw patients away from him, the practitioner. It is surprising that teaching programs have individuals with surplus time on their hands so that they are able to undertake this endeavor.

For the university medical school the goal is trying to protect their source of patients as managed-care plans grow as competitors. Since university medical care includes an overhead expense for the additional cost of teaching and research facilities, the managed-care plans have not found it in their competitive interest to channel patients toward these teaching hospitals.

The teaching hospitals have trained the practitioners and now find themselves in the position of having to compete against their physian output. The old relationship, which included the referral of the more difficult cases to these institutions by these practitioners, is now nearing an end.

The hospitals are running scared and none is more scared than the teaching institutions. Recently, I attended a meeting related to ensuring fairness in making organs available for transplant. After this high-minded discussion I found myself on a downtown street filled with passersby. I was distracted by a recorded message being blared onto the street from a storefront window: ". . . you need a convenient place to get your physical examination. Here we have the ability to do blood chemistries, see a physician, and ensure that you get high-quality care. Please see the receptionist inside to register."

I was being approached for my medical care before I could even get home. I looked at the storefront window to see who was the promoter. In gold and black letters across the window it said, "Downtown Medical Facility for the University Medical Center."

Medicine Benefits from Hard Workers

Just like baseball teams the medical profession is made up of people with varying talents. Some have a propensity to make errors and identify with their own welfare and disregard for their fellow players. The dedication to training the young and the sacrifice they are willing to make to do so also varies.

For a "400 hitter" we'll take Leonard Goldner, professor of orthopaedic surgery at Duke University, now retired. The work machine that was implanted in Leonard still runs in retirement. In Durham he is busy writing papers, taking dedicated interest in his grandchildren and his former patients, and spending time with his wife, who has understood him all these years. The individuals he trained and the students he educated are clustered in North Carolina. From there the Duke representatives have gone over the face of the United States and foreign countries.

Len was a working machine whose motor did not stop until the day's work was done. When I was visiting Duke Medical School as a teacher, I was picked up at the Durham airport by his associate, James Urbaniak, a former Duke football player. I was shown the orthopaedic service, introduced to the residents, and allowed to shower down before Leonard came in that night from Chicago.

Rounds began with all the residents and medical students at 9:00 P.M. Dr. Goldner came in as they started, white with the stress of carrying two briefcases bulging with papers.

Len barely stopped to take his coat off. Each patient was given detailed attention. I kept up with the tail end of the parade, fighting off the tendency to go to sleep that attacks a driver who has been going too long on the road. At 11:30 we had seen the patients and I felt that now I could return to the hotel. Not so. Now we sat in the conference room and the residents presented the patients who were on the operating schedule for tomorrow. Tomorrow was Saturday, a day Leonard found he preferred since no other service was operating. Six rooms were scheduled all day.

I trailed him that Saturday from room to room only slightly refreshed with a few hours' sleep. He was a detailed operator, who artfully separated tissues and did what was required, going over the procedure in detail to make sure it was right. Although Leonard went between two rooms of his own, he also glanced in the other rooms to critique the procedure of other surgeons.

There was no detail he would not stop for, no X ray he would not review, no question he would not answer. He was dogged in his pace as others began to slow down. At nine o'clock that night I was taken to dinner and then dropped into bed thankful that I had survived.

Sunday morning began at 8:00 A.M. There were more teaching rounds where the visiting professor was asked to comment on the work presented. When Leonard disagreed, which was often, he was always courteous. He may have disagreed with others' opinions, but he was always willing to listen.

These presentations went on all morning and did not stop at an appointed hour, but only after all the patients had been seen and discussed, which turned out to go until noon. The residents and I were packed into cars and taken to Len's home, where the dedicated woman who understood all this had sandwiches and tea to revive us.

The residents explained to me that the residency training was an indeterminate number of years. The end was announced when Dr. Goldner determined that the resident was done to his satisfaction. I gathered that there was a certain sense of deliverance when this occurred. There was no resentment of these extra years. Being at Goldner's side was a learning experience, which was appreciated for its golden opportunity. The attachment of the physicians who were trained at Duke was such that it carried over into postgraduate clubs and meetings. It registered in this group as a massive applause for the experience.

On Monday I trailed Dr. Goldner through a full day of seeing patients in the clinic. A good percentage of these were children for whom Len had instant interest and understanding. The afternoon ended with extraordinary patients who had been long-suffering with their condition and frequently had been treated elsewhere. These required detailed medical detective work to get to an understanding of what was going on. The bulldog tenacity of this man came to the front now as others became fatigued trying to reach the answer. Patients came a long way to get this kind of solution to their disease condition. Long hours of surgery might be scheduled as a result.

My father had visited Duke when Leonard was a young staff man. He told me years later that he'd found Dr. Goldner the outstanding young man in orthopaedics at that time and he had seen them all.

Tuesday, Leonard saw private patients so that he could earn a salary to live on. We went through that morning together, and in the afternoon he drove me to the airport. He was going back to Chicago. I returned to Pittsburgh and fell asleep for the entire flight.

Years later, when I needed someone to add to our pediatric orthopaedic service, I found Tim Ward just getting through his training with Dr. Goldner. He had absorbed the work ethic, had the surgical skills, and was dedicated to his patients. It was like transplanting a genie in a bottle; when I uncorked it, a hard-working "400 hitter" popped out and has not stopped.

Fundamentals Still Matter in Efficient Medical Practice

The diagnostic approach is fundamental to medicine. If it does not occur, then treatment is poorly founded. With no real diagnosis, treatment is perhaps inaccurate and unnecessary and certainly results in delay in achieving relief for the patient. A model for the medical detective who became the prototype of the diagnostic physician was translated into a character that fired our imagination. The character was Sherlock Homes. The author who created him was a medical student in Edinburgh whose teacher, a professor of medicine, had demonstrated what keen observation and accurate history-taking could infer about the patient. A. Conan Doyle, himself, was a physician who used the diagnostic method to create the master detective's problem-solving approach. This illustrates what physical examination and history-taking could do to make a diagnosis. It really is the first place to turn before the use of expensive diagnostic machinery.

Medicine is beset by substitute approaches in which diagnosis, which requires so much education, is put in second place to a treatment approach. Thus we have chiropractic, osteopathy, physical therapy, the baths of magical spring waters, heat, light, and electric currents. When a disease entity is present, reliance on a treatment approach without diagnosis can lead to disaster. It is amazing how much must be learned in anatomy, physiology, pathology, bacteriology, and the interpretation of diagnostic imprints such as X-ray films to become a good diagnostician. The methods of physical examination should come before tests or the tests will be poorly chosen. In simple terms, if physical examination discloses a mass in the palm of the hand then an X ray of that area is indicated, not a CAT scan of the whole body.

The more an HMO or other managed-care type of health care insurance shifts the care and entry into the system to poorly trained individuals, the more expensive becomes the process. This has been proven in the past but with the practice of medicine in the hands of lay administrators it looks like it will have to be proven again. When our medicine treats complaints rather than disease processes and uses computerized tomography instead of physical examination we will have trouble keeping our health care at a high level of efficiency and low in cost.

Specialization Is Necessary in Medical Practice

Specialization came about because the knowledge necessary to practice sound medicine is infinitely large in volume and requires great skill to use. A physician with a generalist background could not furnish all the answers. Patients sought out those who could provide answers and who could diagnose the disease causing the patient's complaint. From that point it became easier to furnish treatment that was efficient and creative.

It is strange, but diagnosis and treatment that goes to the heart of the problem is actually cheaper. Anyone who goes every week to the chiropractor for a treatment and who has been doing this for six months without getting rid of the problem can appreciate the truth of this statement.

Managed care tries to limit access to the care of the specialists allegedly for economic reasons. This is done by middle-management individuals unfamiliar with what medicine is and how it works for the good of the patient. The health management of the patient has been fitted into plans designed by novices as related to the practice of medicine. The only way we are going to become familiar with what we need in order to have good and efficient patient care is for those who have been in this profession to publicize who has been working for the patient and what their motivation has been.

Deteriorating Health Care—Progressing Fast

Changes to cause the deterioration of health care are occurring faster than one can write about them. In my former hospital the orthopaedic clinic furnishes a chiropractor or a physiotherapist based primarily on reimbursement. The addition of these treatment areas to a diagnosis and treatment clinic occurs because Blue Cross will reimburse the chiropractor or physiotherapist but not the orthopaedist (read that as specialist) physicians. Economics, not the welfare of the patient, is the guiding influence in these rules.

The Internal Revenue Service challenges the growth of preferred provider organizations (PPOs) who could attract managed-care contracts and patients. The Health Management Organizations (HMOs) are not challenged in this way. The PPO is an amalgamation of physicians and hospitals but is not to be under physician control. The physicians are held to a membership of 20 percent of the PPO board. Federal regulations insist that physicians should have an equal share of the expenses, but the physicians' say in how the organizations are run is sharply limited. The capital necessary and the losses and profits are split fifty-fifty.

It is difficult for PPOs (Preferred Physician Organizations) to compete, although in terms of medical standards the

PPO may be superior. The PPO is seen as acting as a monopoly by those who are government watchdogs. Health care as we have known it is disappearing. You may say that doctors made too much money anyway, and it is certainly true that they will make less in the future. What is being threatened that hurts is the patient's access to high standards of medical care when it is needed.

My friend has a Blue Cross Select policy, which reads as if the old standards of care were being preserved. He is a physician and works at a suburban hospital. He needed routine lab work preliminary to a visit to his doctor. This proved to be a real undertaking. The laboratory work could only be reimbursed if it was done in a corporate laboratory called Med-Check. On Saturday my friend had some free time to get this done, but Med-Check is closed on Saturdays. On weekdays my friend's day began at 7:00 A.M. before Med-Check opened.

As a physician he passed by the laboratory in the hospital every day, but the hospital laboratory had no contract with Blue Cross. He was effectively blocked from participating in a way that would get his laboratory tests reimbursed by Blue Cross.

Blue Cross did not make a profit in decades past, but handled reimbursement funds with a 5 percent overhead. Now that it is a profit-making corporation like other managed-care plans, it is aggressively competing with these plans. The next step has now appeared on the horizon. The move is to offer savings to an employee benefit program in return for becoming the sole provider.

The biggest employers are pushing for savings in their employee health care bill. Blue Cross, in order to make the sale, will lower its cost to the buyer in return for freezing out other managed-care plans, such as Health America. By offering big savings in return for coverage of the entire employee group, Blue Cross is choking out choice for the employee. There are those who argue that the projected savings will not be realized in this move. The ideal for the patient is choice at the consumer level of a combination of economies and quality health care. The old role of Blue Cross was that of administrating claims that the representative of the employees (unions or businesses) paid out of their pocket as part of the cost of doing business. Managed-care plans seek a monopoly as a way of doing business in order to freeze out competition.

As the exclusive insurer, managed-care plans can seek a lessened cost from the hospitals and physicians. This also markedly directs where the patient goes for care. Choice has become limited and some talents and facilities in the community are denied by the patient's inability to get reimbursement when they use them.

Other forces are shaping medical care and the selection of medical care plans. Large hospitals and university hospitals are now worried about being frozen out of the patient flow in their community. If the insuring plan selects small, lesser-cost hospitals, it is not going to cover all of the patients' complaints.

Managed care is a business. The decisions regarding the care are made with the need of the business in mind. Those decisions must enable the people supplying the contract to survive. The costs must be kept down. The areas that are at risk to get less in this tidy arrangement are the hospitals, the doctors, and you, the patient. The medical services may be impossible to supply at the price that the managed-care organization will pay. We have a national treasure—our health care—which we could lose if we are not vigilant.

Chapter VI
A Solution so We Can Get Sick Again

A Unit Cost for Medical Care

The insurance of a number on a plastic card is already a part of life. The Social Security card can become the patient's health care pass number as well.

The country can be divided into six economic areas, with the cost of housing, the salaries, and the basics of food costs, fuel costs, and clothing costs all entered into the definition of the cost-for-care area. For health care costs, the regions could become New England, Mid-Atlantic, Southeast, Middle West, West, and Far Western states. The divisions would be related to the cost of living in a given area.

This plan is for health care reimbursement using a plastic card. The payment is for a unit health care cost and is related to home address. It is a fee for service rather than a capitation plan. The unit health care cost is derived from the cost of furnishing services by institutions and individual practitioners. The unit-cost definition can be trimmed or raised to conform to averages for the region. An adjudicating body in each region can take up variations and determine the services' worth.

The patients and physicians have already noted that it costs an increased amount to send health care monies to Washington and then have it returned to the region. Both of these moves involve an overhead cost that only subtracts from the monies available for health care in an individual economic region.

Unit costs for a given health care service would vary by many features of service that can be defined. These would include facilities available at an institution. Some of the institutions, in the extent of their facilities, could be likened to small-size cars, others to Cadillacs or Lincolns. The unit cost for a given service could also become a definition of the efficiency of the operation and lead to evaluations of the job being done and of the individuals doing the job. The unit-cost fee could become a means of comparison. The unit-fee number, derived from the performance of the service, may lead to corrections in the way things are done at institutions or to individuals who are out of line. This becomes a means of containing costs.

If, for instance, an uncomplicated obstetrical delivery costs twice as much at one institution as compared to the others, there is now a real check leading to justification of the increased cost or the use of methods to bring the cost into line.

A simple appendectomy at one hospital should have a unit-fee cost comparable to other similar-sized institutions. The unit-fee cost becomes a measure of the efficiency of the institution compared to others in the region. The profit that is made by some formerly nonprofit hospitals now becomes apparent.

Teaching institutions can claim additions to the unit-fee cost that relate to the cost of teaching. Also, hospitals of all types do need to make noncapital expenditures to keep up with progress.

The unit-fee cost extends an influence for economy for the activities associated with medical care over the region.

The office for the region that influences rulings for variations in a region becomes very important. The members will need to be protected from political influence and consist of both lay and medical members.

Each hospital could send a member from its board of directors to evaluate the need for these expenditures. The presentation by the hospital would earn an approval or disapproval rating following this presentation. The final approval would rest with the regional unit-fee health committee. The final approval would also rest on the availability of funds for the capital expenditures.

The unit-fee cost would cover the basic minimal cost to render a given health service. Any cost over and above this unit-fee cost would become a surcharge for the patient. Obviously those who wanted more and could afford it, such as a private room, would pay the additional charge.

A physician who could attract more patients could have an increased income. A certified specialist would have a higher unit fee than a generalist. An initial visit would rate a higher unit fee than a follow-up visit.

Those with nonmedical training who are entering into forms of patient care would have a lower unit fee based on their training. Those who are furnishing treatment modalities on prescription, with repetitious visits by the patient, would have a unit fee commensurate with the service that was being rendered. This would include physiotherapists and chiropractic manipulation, but would exclude those advertising cancer cures and miracle drug administrations that have been judged as unfounded in medical science. The quacks and those with exaggerated claims would have no recourse for reimbursement.

The unit-fee system would have great control over health care costs.

The patient would have free choice of physician or institution. Patients could demand increased service or increased amenities in the service, but would themselves become liable for the increased cost over the service furnished by the unit-fee charge for the region.

Everybody with a Social Security number would be covered for medical care and have free choice to get this care—not a bad goal. This system would threaten the interests of many who are making a profit from medical care. Since health care has to be paid for, it becomes important to determine how this will be done.

Paying for Medical Care

If every man, woman, and child is issued a unit-fee health card for medical care, then who is going to pay for it?

If the public is already paying 30 percent of the national income for health care, it is apparent that there are funds out there. Many organizations are making profits that support themselves, but not medical care costs.

Since the unit fee would be the national system to pay for medical care, the cost has been defined. The reimbursement of these charges, region by region, provides a mechanism for reimbursement.

The funds are going to come from sources that are already paying for health care.

Insurance companies are now selling managed health care plans to organizations of groups, industrial companies, small firms, individual subscribers, trade associations, and employee organizations. This leaves out those who are not associated with any of these plans, are not working, or who choose to take their chances with health care costs. Collectively this is an enormous source of funds. These funds are diverted in part of overhead and profits from the sale of health care plans. This last diversion can provide monies for the cost of health care of those who cannot contribute to their own welfare when a different system is instituted.

The money that many organizations are already paying for the health care of their members or employees can be diverted to the unit-fee citizen organization of their health care region. Not by grabbing these expenditures, but by a health care head tax related to the current expenditure by these groups for medical care. This leaves the uncovered, the aged, and those who fall through the cracks in coverage for whom the increase in efficiency of the system will not be sufficient to cover the costs.

The popularity of any plan to collect funds involuntarily for health care will not be there. Whatever plan is used will have to avoid overhead that diverts funds from the coverage of the health care costs. The first saving that is apparent is to avoid the travel of these funds to the national government, where they will be subjected to changes that favor the aims of various national groups before they are returned.

This leaves open a course for health care regions formed by various states who are grouped together. Each state in a region will have to provide its share of the cost of the health care region.

The method that each state chooses to provide these funds is one of the state's choice. The methods include an increase in the state income tax, a sales tax, a designated health care tax, or a fair plan that has not yet been devised.

The medicine tax, which is national, will be gone, but each state can have a medicine tax that underwrites the population defined as aged. The amount of the tax will be related, among other things, to the unit-fee cost that has been determined for the region to which the state belongs.

The directors of health care corporations for any one geographic area would include representatives of medicine, hospitals, and the public. There would be certified public accountants to conduct continuing studies from which to determine the unit fees.

Ongoing studies would furnish statistics supporting the need or lack of need of more hospital beds and other types of medical care facilities. Like any human endeavor there are all types of maneuvers possible to try and corrupt the system. We have to guard against the machinations of those who would direct the system, but we have to do this in all of society's endeavors. We could readily avoid the presence of an excessive number of hospital beds, which plague our health care system today. A hospital bed costs money to maintain, whether it is occupied or not.

We need to preserve a fee-for-service health care system in order to preserve freedom of choice for the patient. This also preserves an economic stimulus for care providers to provide care at a standard that the public will return to for the care. There is stimulus in this system for physicians to be better educated and more willing to serve.

We keep students in our educational pipeline who will go on to extensive training and who will replenish our supply of outstanding people who give us our excellent medical care.

If we continue our managed-care plans run by insurance companies, we find that great profits are being made by these companies. Medical services are rationed, and there is nothing being put back into the system, so that well-trained individuals to be high-class providers will become scarce.

There needs to be support for medical education and research if we expect to continue to have well-trained physicians and surgeons to turn to when we are sick. The companies selling managed-care policies are abdicating some of their responsibilities to our medical care system. Whatever the plan for medical care for the future, it has to include keeping the pipeline of well-educated and trained providers and researchers still flowing.

A Solution so We Can Get Sick Again

Companies who buy health care plans for their employees care about price. The individuals who buy health insurance care about service. The plan that satisfies the patients is one that guarantees that when they are sick then, as patients, they will get care. The HMO often does not risk being a guarantor of health care. They place that risk on the physician by buying the physician's services with a capitation fee. Now the physician will be paid a guaranteed amount for each patient. The patient may require more services and more laboratory tests than the capitation fee covers. The HMO does not take that risk. The physician is responsible for the care of the patient no matter what it entails. Either the patient will not receive high-level care or the physician will go broke taking care of the patient.

The managers and the CEOs of groups, companies, and organizations are buying the contracts of managed health care plans sold by insurance companies. They are buying because the price is cheap compared to the standard fee-for-service plan that they formerly furnished to the employees or members, and they are being promised the same services. Herein lies the dilemma. As our former world-class health care is remodelled, it is not being replaced at the same level of excellence. When it is gone, it will take a long period of education and training to replace it.

As an illustration, this is how a managed health plan contract affected a battered women's shelter. The shelter formerly had a fee-for-service health plan for its patients and employees. The contract was replaced by a managed-care system. A social service worker at this facility was accustomed to instant service when an emergency arose. The social worker's responsibility was the battered woman, pregnant and bleeding, who now lay on the stretcher in front of her. A call to the office of the managed-care plan was disappointing. The social worker was told that she could not send the bleeding woman to the hospital. Instead, she would have to send her charge to the office of the gatekeeper, who would determine if this was truly an emergency warranting her transportation to the emergency room of the local hospital. Time passed while the plan arranged for the gatekeeper to see her. The situation was desperate, and in the meantime the social worker took it upon herself to take the bleeding woman to the hospital. The social worker would have to use funds from the battered women's shelter facility to get her to immediate care rather than funds supplied by the shelter's insurance.

As another example, a truck driver had a lower limb that had been amputated after a previous accident. He wore an artificial limb and had returned to work. Most recently a new limb had been furnished by a prosthetics firm that had made a contract with the health management plan. The amputee was using the new artificial limb when it gave way with failure of the metal uprights. He fell and fractured his femur again. The truck driver lost confidence in his new artificial limb maker and requested referral to his old brace firm. This was denied by the managed-care firm, and the truck driver was told that he would have to use the firm with whom the HMO had a contract. The truck driver was forced to choose to return to his old prosthetic firm in order to get a new limb. This new limb had to be paid for out of the truck driver's own pocket.

The new health care plan had been purchased at considerably less cost than the previous one. It had now become obvious how it was that they could offer a new health service plan at considerably less cost.

Managed Care Runs into Legal Limitations

Managed-care companies are gaining an increasing share of the health care market. The development of the personnel on the panel of these plans has been high-handed. The physician in a particular specialty who is widely regarded as the best talent available in an area may not be on the panel. The available physicians for the patient may be those with the least training who were having trouble getting access to patients in the private-care world. Since these physicians were losing to their competition in the open market, with referral and free choice, they were the most amenable to lowering rates in order to gain inclusion in the plan. This resettlement of the patient-care area has been influenced to exclude the most talented and best trained. The lowest-rated physicians in the available pool now tend to form the major group in the HMO panel. This is a progressive deterioration in the quality of care.

There is a rise in professional liability claims, not only for the physicians, but for the managed-care company.

These suits are based on the failure to diagnose the patients' condition. Economics has denied the full investigation necessary to come to a diagnosis. The gatekeeper is being recognized as having a real liability as well. There is great pressure on the gatekeeper to reduce the utilization of diagnostic services and to extend the area they will take care of in order to avoid referral to a specialist.

There is a growing world of legal liability for the plan and the gatekeeper. Courts have not taken kindly to what is perceived as the denial of the loss of opportunity for care brought about by economic pressure from the administrators of the management plan.

Pity the family physician caught between two forces. It is hard to be a patient advocate and still stifle the progression of the patient into a care area where a diagnosis would be achieved. Denial of care is a common allegation in the increasing number of lawsuits against managed-care plans. Premature discharge or denial of admission in the first place is going to become an allegation that originates a lawsuit.

The gatekeeper still has to do all that is necessary for proper care and fight for the patient to avoid limiting care by the plan. It is hard to fight your employer and doing so may leave the gatekeeper open to reprisal from the plan.

The other side of the dilemma is the difficulty a gatekeeper has in trying to retain his relationship with the patient when at the same time he is limiting access to specialists, laboratory tests, and hospitals. The explanation that the restrictions are imposed by the patient's insurance company does not make you, the patient, any happier. You only appreciate the fact that limitations are imposed when you run up against them. You thought you bought coverage for your medical care and the maintenance of your health. The coverage the patient has only becomes obvious when sickness occurs.

If there are guidelines for the physician, it makes a great deal of difference in court who wrote them. If they are the profiteers of a managed-care company without using physician input, then the gatekeeper does not have a legal backup.

The gatekeeper is a sitting duck for the lawyer accustomed to use the ability to accuse and win by delineating a possible weakness in the system.

The gatekeeper is rewarded for keeping referrals to the specialist at a minimum. With this carrot in front of the general practitioner and, in many cases a financial penalty for referrals, the possibilty arises that many people who needed a referral to get recognition of a life-threatening condition will not have an opportunity to obtain it. When a condition is unrecognized, then therapy becomes merely a repetitious treatment regime using useless pills or manipulations or repetitious treatments. The gatekeeper may find that exposure in a medical-legal sense goes with the job. The managed-care administration can put up with using the gatekeeper as a sacrificial lamb until the legal judgments begin to reach into the home office. Now the economy of the plan is threatened. The growth in judgments against the gatekeeper and the health plan threatens the gatekeeper approach. It is probably dead. It is probably dead for a lot of good reasons from the patient's point of view. It is probably dead because it denies patients the use of the methods, tools, and skills of specialism in medicine, which were developed over years of training. The gatekeeper is placed in a position that is not tenable from the standpoint of legal security, and the number of volunteers willing to be placed in this position is diminishing.

Managed-Care Solutions

Medical care plans to insure your care are growing because they offer a lower-cost health care contract. They purchase service at 20 to 30 percent less but sell them to you at only 10 percent less. They can pocket the difference. These insurers are making money, and the price of their stock is rising in the marketplace. The cost savings are at the patients' and physicians' expense. What is the right level of care that the patient should expect for his health care dollar? The nurse has been priced out of hospital health care. Some are now used to provide what used to be the patient/doctor interface.

A lesser level of care has been substituted as managed-care plans insure a larger percentage of the population. Please don't get sick until the level of medical care gets defined and the patients know what they are getting.

The executives of managed-care plans have found physicians and some hospitals very naive in the business world. It is a simple world for these executives in which they can easily outmaneuver the physician.

The doctor has become confused as to the aim of the insurance companies putting out managed-health plans. The physicians are easily approached and asked to form groups for whom the health plan will provide patients. The plans will also provide other services for the doctors, which alleviate their expense. These include advertising, sales, business operations and personnel, including billing and finally real estate to work in. One group of physicians met with the president of the plan to put the details of the plan together after they had been given a letter of intent by the plan. The group of physicians in this example numbered over one hundred. They had been drawn by the features of the plan, which included an enlarged patient flow and a lowered overhead. (Most of them were carrying a 50 to 60 percent overhead in their practices.)

At the meeting with the executives of the plan, after furnishing the insurance company with their lowest possible fee at which they were willing to work, the physicians were told that the insurance company was not going to support the formation of their group and its practice. Anger erupted because the physicians had been furnished a letter of intent by the plan. They were told that the letter had been canceled by the insurance plan and was no longer in force.

The physicians were now told that if they wished to become employees of the managed-care plan they could do so. The health care plan would use the prices the physicians had furnished in the billing calculations and would subtract the plan's overhead from that amount. Clever maneuvering of inexperienced physicians had left them with no alternative.

When it comes to dealing with hospitals, the insurance companies forming managed-care plans have a harder time. The board of the hospital is composed of business men who deal in their world. They oversee the negotiations of the hospital administrators. But because medicine is a world that the board finds it hard to communicate with (and does not fully understand) there is room for the insurance company to maneuver.

A small hospital that has enjoyed the services of an excellent staff over the years makes an example that indicates what is going on.

The administrators and a trustee company met with the insurance company. They were one of many hospitals that were similarly approached. The gist of the proposition for each hospital was that the insurance company was going to choose a few of them to become hospitals affiliated with their plan. They were told that they already had 700,000 subscribers and indications were that they would double the number in the next year. The managed-care plan selling to large groups of employees or members of large organizations were clearly offering health care at a reduced cost compared to present contracts. It has been strange that the leaders of these groups did not insist that the level of care be defined. Exactly what is being offered is defined only in general, good-sounding terms. Only experience with the actual operation of the plan clarifies what is really being offered.

In order to compete for the affiliation with the plan, offering large numbers of potential patients, each hospital was asked to furnish the lowest possible cost at which they would be willing to furnish the hospital's services.

In dutiful fashion each group of hospital administrators and their accompanying committee of trustees went home to work out their lowest possible cost. This was submitted like a bid to the health care plan run by the insurance company.

Time went by and each hospital was notified that rather than choosing one among them all, the plan would use each of them, determined by their subscribers who were grouped geographically. The plan had each hospital with a minimal bid that they otherwise might not have gotten. For many of these hospitals it meant discharging employees and limiting services in order to meet the terms that they had offered when they had felt the need to survive in a world that had seen their former patients now being underwritten by the managed-care plan.

It also meant dropping down the level of care that was offered. The least expensive employee was substituted for a better-trained employee in order to contain costs. The physicians had no input in this degradation of services. The patient had no realization that this was occurring. After all, health care is health care; medical services are medical services. Please do not get sick until the true definition of medical services is apparent.

Somebody may be smart enough to realize that if medical care plans are choosing the cheapest providers as their criteria for care, they are choosing the least trained and the most willing to be available. Somebody may be smart enough to realize that the most risk to the ability of medicine and health care facilities to maintain the level of medical care that patients are used to is not the government's efforts to provide national health insurance; it is becoming more evident that it is insurance company health plans driven by the profit motive.

It is assumed that in our country the health care consumer wishes to preserve the high level of health care that made people the world over come to our shores. Incorporating some of the gains lowering costs that managed care has developed, it becomes important that the entire cost reduction be passed on to the consumer. There is no reason why 20 percent of this reduction should go to HMO coffers. It takes a long educational process to develop expert health care providers. The cost savings should keep the pipeline open so that there is training for the specialists and the experts that we need. In a fee-for-service system it is possible to seek specialist care when it is apparent that it is needed. The patient cannot expect the generalist to do everything. Hospital charges should be related to goods and services that are received. The confidence that when patients are sick they have the people and equipment that will give them the best chance to recover has to be there. It looks like there should be a relatively simple solution.

The experts that will form the unit-cost committee will mirror the community and the consumer as well as the various groups providing services. It is not determined by these committees who the consumers should see for their condition. The consumers can see the provider that they feel can have the best chance of providing health care solutions for their condition. They can choose their level of care without having to use a gatekeeper.

There is a control of unit-fee costs by the economic community. Neither the insurance company promoting managed care nor the government determine charges. The physician or the hospital gain by providing services that are sought by consumers. These health care providers are in competition with others to provide these services as a means of controlling costs. Costs are also controlled by determining a unit fee for the economic community as the first basic step.

Providers can meet those increases in cost caused by providing more luxurious services by percentage increases over and above the unit fee. They must gain approval for this increase from the consumer, who is free to go elsewhere to get basic service for a unit fee without any additional costs.

For the population to have the best medical care, the practice of medicine is done by the well-trained physician for the particular problem. The present-day use of primary-care physicians to cover all modalities and situations will have difficulty surviving. The primary-care provider is very uncomfortable trying to cover all facets of disease and all types of conditions. The patient is aware of this. Good medical care cannot be done when the decisions are made over the phone by the health care plan's employee guarding the purse strings.

It surprises many who are unfamiliar with medical practice that many specialists are primary-care providers as well. The orthopaedic surgeon during the office hours sees many patients with skeletal complaints. Many come by referring themselves. Not all need special procedures, but they do need an accurate diagnosis of their condition. This is a one-visit, low-overhead method of dealing with the multitude of patient complaints. It surpasses the administrative overload necessary to carry out a gatekeeper function. This latter function involves two visits and the services of an adjudicating health plan interposed between them. This is not the most efficient attack on this problem that we can devise.

When patients can choose their physician, those most skilled become the most used. If there is anything to education to meet the performance of a task, then the efficiency of the service is increased.

The Growth of Managed Care

The insurance companies' health care plan has reduced costs and the insurance companies are making money. An important reason for the economic growth of managed health care is to diminish services available to the patient. Where these plans are making great profits, a percentage should be returned to society in the form of support for medical research in order to benefit society as a whole and ensure our future medical development and services. Insurance companies selling health care contracts can obtain unit-fee under-writing in the future from the state. The amount that they can charge for handling the contract will be determined by what the public will pay.

Capitation is great for HMOs; they take no risk for increased patient services. The experience of physicians working for employee health plans provided by a hospital is the increasing use of the physician for minor complaints for most patients. The system cannot be freely open without a penalty for the patients' overuse of the service when it is free. This means the interposition of some form of copay from the patient. Even the smallest of charges makes for a deterrent to overuse. In order to handle the multitude of complaints the system will have to use physicians' assistants. These individuals will operate only under the supervision of the physician. This can be efficiently done when both work in the same office but not when they are not working under supervision.

The experience of physicians now is that the insurer-managed health care slows the system. Telephone calls get backed up. Replies to requests allowing the physician to proceed with care are often inordinately delayed. The answers may not advance the care of the patient.

Deficits of the System

The older types of health care insurance cost a family roughly $250 per month per person. A health care foundation has a managed health care plan that is based on capitation. Apparently they now insure one and one-half million people and started out four years ago with a capitation charge of $120 per person, which is now down to $80 per month per person. The patients now have a system of care, but not a doctor. The doctor, if he sees the need for laboratory tests, has to order these tests at his own risk. The capitation fee covered the patient's care no matter what it entailed. The HMO took no risk. Medical care insurance may not cover the provision of medical care.

Physicians are changing in their attitude toward the approach to medical practice. The modern medical student wants four to six weeks of vacation time. They are seeking a structured work day in which they work only six to eight hours per day and then pass the baton on to someone else. Forty percent of the students are female and they want a more structured life style so that they can have a family. The patients are accepting this new system of medical practice because of finances. The remuneration for primary-care physicians has risen and specialists' income has dropped. All physicians will be in a narrow band of income in the future. There will be less cost and less service. The ultimate question will be what do patients demand. This demand will only be truly expressed when there has been sufficient experience with the new system. This book has been written from the standpoint that as patients we may not realize what we have lost in excellence in health care until it is no longer available. Experience may lead to increased demand and we may not have those trained to supply it. We have to keep good guys available for our care.

We can have the best of both worlds if we plan intelligently. We have to put incentives into the system in order to regain high-class medical care. As in many other countries, we may find that higher classes of medical care are available only to the elite. A physician from medicine as it was practiced in times past wants necessary medical care available to everyone.

Some of the means of maintaining this state of affairs are apparent, others will exist as we sense our losses. Don't get sick until the ship is running on an even keel and not listing to port.

With a unit fee for costs and regional underwriting of these costs, we will get medical care for everyone. At the same time we will keep government and insurance companies out of the business and eliminate the managed-care profit. Rationing medical care and reducing the level of care and choice available to the consumer will be gone. This is essential so that all patients can enter a medical care situation with confidence when we are sick.